SHASTA OF THE WOLVES

THE BABY WOLF-BROTHERS SAT IN A ROW . . . SNIFFING WITH
THEIR PUPPY NOSES *Page 16*

SHASTA OF THE WOLVES

BY

OLAF BAKER

ILLUSTRATIONS BY
CHARLES LIVINGSTON BULL

NEW YORK
DODD, MEAD AND COMPANY
1942

Printed in U. S. A.

CONTENTS

CHAPTER		PAGE
I	THE WOLF-CHILD	3
II	THE COMING OF SHOOMOO	15
III	SHASTA COMES VERY NEAR BEING EATEN BY A BEAR	29
IV	THE END OF THE FIGHT	47
V	GOMPOSH, THE WISE ONE	57
VI	SHASTA SINGS THE WOLF CHORUS	69
VII	SHASTA JOINS THE WOLF PACK	87
VIII	THE VOICE THAT WAS GOOHOOPERAY	99
IX	THE COMING OF KENNEBEC	109
X	HOW SHASTA HID IN TIME	131
XI	SHASTA'S RESTLESSNESS AND WHAT CAME OF IT	139
XII	SHASTA SEES HIS REDSKIN KINDRED	151
XIII	THE BULL MOOSE	177
XIV	SHASTA LEAVES HIS WOLF KIN	205
XV	HOW SHASTA FOUGHT MUSHA-WUNK	223
XVI	THE DANGER FROM THE SOUTH	235
XVII	SHASTA GOES SCOUTING	249
XVIII	THE WOLVES AVENGE	267

ILLUSTRATIONS

PAGE

The baby wolf-brothers sat in a row . . . sniffing
with their puppy noses . . . . . . *Frontispiece*

Very deliberately and slowly, he came down the
slope towards Shasta and sat down on his
haunches 60

What was that driving furiously up the long steeps
of the dawn? 126

With a harsh bellow of rage and anguish he plunged
into the underwood 200

THE WOLF-CHILD

SHASTA OF THE WOLVES

CHAPTER I

THE WOLF-CHILD

IT was the old she-wolf Nitka that came running lightly along the dusk. Though she had a great and powerful body, with a weight heavy enough to bear down a grown man, her feet made no sound as they came padding through the trees. She had been a long way, travelling for a kill, because at home the wolf-babies were very hungry and gave her no peace. They were not well-behaved babies at all. Whatever mischief there was in the world seemed to be packed tight into their little furry bodies. They played and fought and worried each other till they grew hungry again, and then they fell upon their mother like the little ravening monsters that they were. But Nitka bore it all patiently, as a kind old mother should, and only gave them a smack occasionally, when their behaviour was beyond everything for naughtiness.

Now, as she came running through the trees she drank in the air thirstily through her long nose. For it was her nose that brought her news of the forest, telling her what creatures were abroad, and whether there was a chance of a kill. This evening the air was full of smells, and heavy with the heat of the long summer day; but many of them were wood smells, tree smells, green smells; not the scent of the warm fur and the warm flesh and the good blood that ran in the warm bodies and made them spill the secret of themselves along the air. And it was this warm, red, running smell for which Nitka was so thirsty, and of which there was so little spilt upon the creeping dusk. Yet now and then a delicate whiff of it would come, and Nitka would sniff harder, swinging her head into the wind. And sometimes it grew stronger and sometimes weaker, and sometimes would cease altogether, swallowed up in the scent of the things that were green. And then, all of a sudden, the smell came thick and strong, flowing like a stream along the drift of the air.

In the wild, your scent is yourself. What

[4]

you smell like, that you are. And so, accordingly as the wind blows, you spill yourself, even against your will, either backwards or forwards, on the currents of the air.

Nitka increased her pace, and as she ran the smell grew sweeter and stronger, and made her mad for the kill. It was not long before her sharp eyes gave her sight of a deer feeding in an open glade. Nitka stooped her long body to the earth, and began to stalk her prey. All about her the forest seemed to hold back its breath.

It was no noise which Nitka made which betrayed her presence. She herself came stooping nearer like a shadow on four feet. And as it was up-wind that she came, she spilt herself upon the air backwards, not forwards, to the deer. Yet something there was which seemed to give it warning beyond sound, or sight, or smell.

It stopped feeding, and lifted its head. For a moment or two it stood as still as an image carved in stone; yet, as Nitka knew well, it was the stillness of warm flesh that paused before it fled. She gathered her legs under her for the deadly spring. The deer turned its head quickly, and saw a long grey shadow launch itself through the dusk. It was the last leaping shadow the deer would ever see. For the law of the forest is a stern and unpitying one—the law of Hunger, and the law of Desire.

When Nitka had finished her kill, and satisfied her hunger, she thought of the babies at home. They were too small yet for flesh food, so it was no use carrying any back to them. Nevertheless they would be wanting their supper badly, and she must go and give it to them if she would have any quiet in her mind. So she trotted through the forest, having first buried some pieces of the deer where she would know where to find them.

The cave in which her cubs were waiting was far away, for she had travelled many miles, but her instinct told her how to find it easily again, and she made a straight line for it, loping along towards the hills. She was going down-wind now, and did not catch a scent of the things in front. But as she had had her kill, that did not matter. There was one thought in her old wise head, and that thought was home.

But before she reached it, she lit upon a strange thing. It lay right in her path—a small brown bundle that now and then set up a thin wail. Nitka observed it carefully, then ran round to the leeward of it to pick up its scent the better. With strange things she always did this. You never knew what a strange thing might do before your nose could give you warning. As she circled, she came upon another smell which she had smelled before—the scent of man, of which she was afraid. But it was a trail several hours old, and was growing a little stale. Nitka crept up to the peculiar bundle. She sniffed at it hard, then turned it over gently with her paw. As she did so, it stirred a little and whimpered. The smell was the smell of man, but the whimper was that of a cub. Nitka distrusted the smell, but the whimper was good. She was not hungry now, but there were the hungry babies at home. She must not delay any longer. She caught up the bundle by the loose skin that covered it, and started off again.

[7]

She had to go more slowly now, because of the bundle, and when at last she reached the cave upon the mountain-side, the night had fallen. Dark though it was, the baby wolves were awake, and ready for a famous meal; but in the odd bundle which their mother dropped inside the mouth of the den they were not interested enough to find out what it was. When they had had their supper they fell fast asleep, and when the rising moon cast a glimmer into the cave, you might have seen an old mother wolf and a family of cubs all snuggled up together and very fast asleep.

But in the morning, when they woke up, there was another cub, a cub whose clothes were not of fur, but of a strange covering which they would have called Indian blanket if they had had any word for such a thing in their furry language. However, they speedily took to worrying this odd blanket; and presently off it came and was found to be no skin at all, but only a loose cover that tore to pieces beautifully, and made you cough when you tried to swallow it. Inside, the baby had

[8]

another skin that was of a reddish brown and very soft. They began to worry that also, hoping it might come off too, but it stuck fast to what was underneath, as is the way with such skins, being specially prepared to stick, and the baby inside it began to squeal like mad.

For some reason or other, the baby did not bite back again. It just lay on its back, and waved fat arms and legs in the air. That hurt nobody, so the little wolves rolled it over and over, and tried to take pieces out of its arms and legs, and thought it was quite the biggest joke they had had in all their lives. Only the new baby did not have a sense of humour, and refused to enter into the fun. It only squealed louder and louder, and actually squeezed water out of its little eyes!

Then, all at once, without any warning whatever, Nitka put a stop to the fun by cuffing her babies right and left; and so the new baby did not have to cry alone, but was joined by all the little wolves, yelping with fear and pain. So from that time onward they learned slowly that the new baby was not to be bitten just for fun, but was somehow or other a little naked brother who had left his coat behind him in the outside world.

If you had asked Nitka why she had taken the baby's part, I don't believe she could have told you. All she knew was that there was a feeling inside her that this odd thing she had found in the forest was to be protected from harm.

That was in the early days of little Shasta's life. He was so tiny that he soon grew used to the difference between living among the wolves and living among his own kind. And soon he forgot even the dim thing he once remembered, and thought there was no life but the life of the cave where always it was shadowy and cool even in the hottest summer day. And he learned to play with the little wolves, his brothers, and wrestle and box with them, and go tumbling all over the cave floor with never a squeal. Only sometimes when the play seemed to grow too rough, and old Nitka thought he was having a bad time of it, she would rescue him from his playmates, and give everybody a general smacking all round:

[10]

and then there would be peace for a little time.

So that is how it came to pass that Shasta learnt the language of the wolves, and of the other animals—and indeed for a time knew no other—and understood what they said and thought, and even felt, when there was no need of any words.

And all this knowledge was of great use afterwards, and was the saving of his life, as you shall presently be told.

THE COMING OF SHOOMOO

CHAPTER II

THE COMING OF SHOOMOO

NOW the first great day in little Shasta's wolf life was the day when he left the cave for the first time and came out into the open world. He didn't know why he was to go out, nor what going out really meant. All he knew was that, suddenly, there was a movement of all the cubs towards the place where the light came from, and that it seemed natural for him to follow the movement.

When he crawled outside, the sunlight hit him smack in the face like a hot white hand, and then, when he got over that, the world swam in upon his little brain in the way of a coloured dream. It was a very splendid dream, in which everything was new and strange and beautiful beyond all words to describe. The baby wolf-brothers sat in a row

[15]

and blinked out at the dream, sniffing at it
with their puppy noses because of the instinct
within them that even dreams must be smelt
if you would find out what they are. And it
seemed to them to be a very good dream, smelling of grass and flowers, and of hot rocks, and
of the sharp scent which the pine trees loose
on the summer air. And there, on a rising
piece of ground, sat the old wolf-mother, also
smelling the good world, only that, besides the
smell of the trees and rocks, she could distinguish those other odours of living creatures
which drift idly down the wind.

Shasta, a little way behind his wolf-brothers,
sat down too. When a large curious dream
comes it is better to sit and watch what it will
do; otherwise, if you begin to walk about in
it, you may fall over something, and come to
a bad end! So Shasta sat and blinked at the
thing, and waggled his fingers and his toes.
He smelt at the thing also, and to him, as to
the others, it seemed a good and pleasant smell,
and he gurgled with delight. The sound he
made was so funny that the cubs turned round
to see what was happening. But when they

saw that it was only the foster-brother being odd as usual, they turned away again and went on smelling at the world.

High up above his head, Shasta saw something very white and hot. It was so dazzling that he couldn't look up at it for more than a moment at a time, and because the thing hurt his eyes, and set queer round plates dancing in front of them when he looked away, he gave up looking at it. Yet always he was conscious that it was there—the hot white centre to this curious dream. And once he lifted a little hairy hand to give it a cuff for being so hot and silly; only, somehow, the hand didn't quite reach, and when he tried a little higher, he overbalanced and fell over on his back.

This was a signal for the cubs to rush at him and have a game. So for a long time, Shasta cuffed at them and wrestled with them, and sometimes got the better of them, and sometimes was badly beaten and worried like a rat. Of course neither he nor they had any idea that this delightful scuffling and cuffing was really the beginning of their education, and that their muscles were being trained and

[17]

their limbs strengthened for their battle with the world when they should be grown up, and babies no longer.

Suddenly, as if by magic, the play stopped dead, with Shasta and the cubs locked in a fierce embrace. Old Nitka never made a sound, nor any outward sign, which ordered the play to cease. Yet in a twinkling the cubs were back into the den, while Nitka had risen from her point of observation, with her eyes set hard to the north. Shasta sat up and stared. The last wolf-brother was wobbling his fat body into the cave's mouth. Shasta felt, in some odd unexplained way, that he ought to follow, and that it was because Nitka had willed it, that the cubs had gone in. Yet because he was a man-baby, and not a wolf-cub, he stayed where he was and stared at his foster-mother with large and wondering eyes. But Nitka did not look at him. Her eyes were far away over the tops of the spruces and pines—far away to a certain spot where a level rock jutted out from the great "barren" that stretched like a roof along the windy top of the world. If Shasta had followed the direction of Nitka's eyes, he would have seen what looked like the form of a large timber-wolf lying crouched upon the rock, with his nose well into the wind. Only Shasta had no eyes for anything but Nitka. He had never seen her look so fierce before. All her great body was stiffened as if with steel springs. Just above her tail her hair was raised, as is the way when a wolf or dog is roused for fight; and in her gleaming eyes, burning like dull coals, there was a green, unpleasant light. Shasta could not tell what ailed his foster-mother. Only, in a dim way, he felt that something was amiss. And the feeling made him uncomfortable, as when a grown-up person says nothing to you, but has a slap ready in the hands.

Presently Nitka saw the other wolf slip off the rock and disappear in the spruce scrub at its base. And then, as before, she let herself down, and the bristles flattened above her tail. She seemed to rest in her body, and to give up all her bones to the warmth of the summer afternoon. Near by, the stream fell down the hill-side with a sleepy murmur, and

the grasshoppers chirruped in the grass.
There was nothing to be seen except, high up
in the air, a sweep of slow wings that bore
Kennebec, the great eagle, in his solemn circles above the canyon at the foot of the mountain. Kennebec was a mighty person in his
own world, as many a wolf and mountain sheep
knew to their cost. Many and many a lamb
and wolf-cub had gone to the feeding of Kennebec's children in their dizzy eyrie built
among the steeples of the rocks. But as long
as Kennebec kept to his own canyon, and did
not cast a wicked eye upon her babies, Nitka
did not worry about him, and had all her
senses on the watch for danger nearer at hand.
For in spite of all her look of outward lazi-
ness, every nerve that she had, every muscle
of her strong body, was ready at a moment's
notice to send her flying at any creature which
dared to venture within striking distance of
the den.

For a long time nothing happened. Then
Nitka growled softly, looking at Shasta as she
did so. Now Shasta knew perfectly well that
the growl was meant for him. Up to the pres-

ent he had been disobedient, though he didn't quite know how. Nitka wished him to return to the cave with the cubs, and Shasta, though he felt some instinct telling him to go, could not understand what it meant, and so remained exactly where he was. And so far Nitka had been very patient. She had simply gone on wanting him to get back into safety, but she had not looked or spoken. The soft growl, rumbling down there in her deep throat, was not a pleasant thing to hear. It sent a thrill down Shasta's little spine. He began to feel dreadfully uncomfortable, and to wish that he was safe inside the cave. Yet still he did not move, because the man-cub inside his heart was not inclined to bow down before the wolves.

Again Nitka growled, this time louder than before. And to make it more pointed, she looked at Shasta as she growled. He had never seen her look at him like that before. The light in her eyes was not at all agreeable. There was a threat in it, as to what she might do if Shasta did not obey. He began to edge away towards the cave. After he had gone

two or three yards he stopped. This behaviour of Nitka was so curious that he wanted
to find out what it meant. Something was
going to happen. Without in the least knowing what it might be, Shasta felt that something was in the air. But there was no re-
sisting that look in Nitka's eyes. With a
whimpering cry, Shasta scrambled to the entrance of the cave. Once inside the den's
mouth, however, his courage came to him
again, and he turned to look back.

As he peeped, he saw the form of a huge
grey wolf glide into the open space. Nitka
herself was large, but this other wolf was
nearly half as big again and much more for-
midable. His great limbs and deep chest were
wonderful to see. Between his shoulders was
a dark patch of hair which was thicker than
the rest of his coat, and, when the winter came,
would become a sort of mane. He stood
nearly three feet high at the shoulders—a giant
of his breed.

As to Nitka herself, she was plainly in a
rage. The hackles on her back were raised;
her body was crouched low as if to leap, her

[22]

limbs were bent under her like powerful springs to send the whole weight of her great body hurling through the air; while, if her eyes had shone threateningly before when she looked at the disobedient Shasta, now they gleamed with a green light that seemed like living flame.

So the two wolves stood facing each other, the huge stranger not seeming to like the look of things, with Nitka snarling defiance at him, and prepared to give her very life in the defence of her cubs.

Shasta, peeping timidly out from the mouth of the cave, felt certain that some terrible thing was about to happen. He was terrified by two things: first, by the mysterious coming of the stranger wolf, then by the awful anger of Nitka, which, if once let loose, must surely tear the new world to pieces, hot white centre and all! Behind him, in the cave, the cubs were motionless and made no sound. They huddled closely together as if they knew, though they could not see it, that, out there in the sunlight, a strange thing was happening with which it would be fatal to interfere. So there they huddled, and pressed their fat furry bodies against each other, and tried to be comforted by each other's fat and fur.

Then Shasta, looking out boldly, saw a very odd thing. He saw the he-wolf make a step towards Nitka with a sort of friendly whine in his throat, and Nitka, instead of springing at him, remained crouched where she was. And although she kept on growling, and saying the most dreadful things as before, somehow or other she seemed less vicious, and the green glare was softening in her eyes. Seeing this, the other wolf grew bolder, and drew closer step by step.

It was a very slow approach, as if the giant he-wolf was fully aware that any sudden action of his would bring Nitka on him like a fury, with those long fangs of hers bared to strike. And then at last the two wolves were so close together that their noses touched. And in this touch of their noses, and the silent conversation which followed, everything was explained and understood, and made clear for the future.

So that was how Shasta saw the return of

[24]

The Coming of Shoomoo

Shoomoo, the father of his foster-brothers, and Nitka's lawful mate. After that Shoomoo became a recognized person in the world who came and went mysteriously, never saying when he was going, nor telling you where when he had come back. Only that did not matter in the least. The really big thing was that when father Shoomoo did come back, he seldom returned empty-handed, or I should say empty-mouthed, since a wolf uses his mouth as a carry-all, instead of his paws.

SHASTA COMES VERY NEAR BEING EATEN BY A BEAR

CHAPTER III

THE weeks and the months went by.
Only Shasta did not know anything
about time, and if the months ticked
themselves off into years, he took no account
of them. Each month he became more and
more wolf-like, and less and less like a human
child. And because he wore no clothes, hair
began to grow over his naked body, so that
soon there was a soft brown silky covering all
over him, and the hair of his head fell upon
his shoulders like a mane. And as he grew
older much knowledge came to him, which is
hidden from human folk, or which perhaps
they have forgotten in their building of the
world. He learnt not only how to see things
very far off, and clearly, as if they were near,
but he learnt also to bring them close by smell-

ing, to know what manner of meat they were. And if his nose or his eyes brought him no message, then his ears gave him warning, and he caught the footsteps that creep stealthily along the edges of the night. And he learnt the difference between the three hunting calls of the wolf: the howl that is long and deep, and which dies among the spruces, or is echoed dismally among the lonely crags; the high and ringing voice of the united pack, on a burning scent; and that last terrible bark that is half a howl, when the killing is at hand.

Yet it was not only of the wolves that Shasta learnt the speech of the Wild. He knew the things the bears rumbled to each other as they went pad-padding on enormous feet. Of the black bears he had no fear, but for the grizzlies he had a feeling that warned him it was wiser to keep out of their way. The feeling was not there in the beginning, but it grew after a thing that happened one never-to-be-forgotten day.

He had been sleeping in the cave during the hot hours, and woke up as the light began to yellow in the waning of the afternoon. He

[30]

stretched his little hairy arms and legs with a great feeling of rest and of happiness. He felt so well and strong in every part of him that the joyful life inside him seemed bubbling up and spilling over. He was alone in the cave, for his wolf-brothers were now grown up and were gone out into the world. Sometimes, at sundown or dawn, he heard them sing the strange wolf-song—the song that is as old as the world itself—or a familiar scent would drift to him, as he sat in the entrance of the cave, and he would know it for the sweet good smell of some wolf-brother as he passed across the world. And sometimes Shasta would lift his child's voice into that wild, unearthly wolf-song that is so very old.

This afternoon, something seemed to call Shasta to go out into the sun. Nitka had made him understand that it was not safe for him to go far from the cave when she was away. Now she was out hunting, and Shoo-moo was off on one of his mysterious journeys, nobody knew where, so there was all the more need for Shasta to stay close at home. Shasta did not see why he should remain in the dull den all the time that his foster-parents were away. Besides, were not his wolf-brothers all far out in the world? Perhaps he might fall in with one of them, and sniff noses together for the sake of old times. He determined to go out and try.

As he passed out, he heard the Blue Jays scolding in the trees.

Now there is a rule which all wise forest folk observe. It is this: When the Blue Jay scolds, look out!

Sometimes, of course, the Blue Jays simply scold at each other, because somebody has taken somebody else's grub, or just because they have a falling-out for fun; but the wise wild folk pay no attention to this, knowing it to be what it is. And when the Blue Jays scold in a peculiar manner, then the wise ones know that there is danger afoot, and that you must keep a sharp look out.

Now, although Shasta was so young, he was quite old enough to understand the difference in the sounds. Unfortunately, this afternoon he was in a mad mood, and he just didn't care! He saw the autumn sun bright on the rocks at the den's mouth; he saw the glimmer of the blue over the tall tops of the pines. High above the canyon, a dark blob circled slowly against the sky. Far off though it was, Shasta saw that it was Kennebec, the great eagle, who was lord of all the eagles between the mountains and the sea. Shasta watched him for a little while making wide circles on his mighty sweep of wing. Then he ran up the mountainside, and, as he ran, the Blue Jays scolded more and more.

If Shasta had not been in so mad a mood, he would have known by the chatter of the Jays that the danger was coming up-hill. Also, if he himself had not been running down-wind, he would have smelt what the danger was creeping up behind. But the something that had seemed to call him in the cave was calling to him now from the high rocks. So on he climbed, careless of what might be going on below. He climbed higher and higher. Close by one of the big rocks a birch-tree hung itself out into the air. When he reached it he stopped to look back.

Down at the edge of the forest he saw a thing

that made him shiver. From between the shadowy trunks of the pine-trees, the shape of a huge Grizzly swung out into the sun. It came on steadily up the mountain, its nose well into the wind. Shasta knew that he himself was doing the fatal thing; he was spilling himself into the wind, and even now the Grizzly was eating him through his nose!

By this time Shasta was very frightened. He looked this way and that, to see how to escape. He knew that he could not get back to the cave in time, for it lay close to the Grizzly's upward path, and already the bear was half-way there. The moving of his great limbs sent all his fur robe into ripples that were silver in the sun. He was coming at a steady pace. And, if he wanted to quicken it, Shasta knew with what a terrible quickness those furry limbs could move. As for himself, his wolf-training had taught him to run very swiftly, but he ran in a stooping way, using his hands as well as his feet. Only he doubted whether his swiftness could save him from the Grizzly over the broken ground. And far away over the canyon Kennebec swept his vast circles as calmly as though nothing was happening, because all went so very well in the blue lagoons of the air. Nothing was happening up there; but here upon the Bargloosh everything was happening, and poor little Shasta felt that everything was happening wrong.

In his terrible fear Shasta started to run up the mountain. As he ran, he looked back. He saw to his horror that the Grizzly had seen him and had also started to run. Up the rocky slopes came the terrible pad-pad of those cruel paws. And Shasta knew well that the paws had teeth in them; many cruel teeth to each paw. And still Shasta went darting upward, running swiftly like a mountain-fox.

As he ran, a thought came into his head. If he could circle down the mountain, he might hide behind the rocks till the Grizzly had passed, and so reach the cave in time. For he had the sense to know that although a Grizzly is more than a match for wolves in the open, it thinks many times before it will attack them in their den.

U. S. 864025

Again Shasta looked back. He saw that the Grizzly was gaining upon him. He turned

[35]

swiftly among the boulders to the left, dodging as he went so as to be out of sight of his enemy. The longer he could keep up the flight the more chance there was that either Nitka or Shoomoo might return. He ran on wildly, the terror in him, like the Grizzly behind, gaining ground.

He saw the long mountainside stretching out far and far before him to the northwest. He looked eagerly to see if any grey shadows should be moving eastwards along it—the long, gliding shadows that would be his wolf-parents coming home. But nothing broke the lines of grey boulders that lay so still along the slopes. All the great mountains seemed dead or asleep. Nothing living moved. Shasta ran on and on, looking fearfully backwards now and then, and expecting every moment to see the form of the great Grizzly come bounding over the rocks. Far below him in the timber he heard the screaming of the Jays. There was a fresh tone in the cry. Before, it had been a scolding of the bear: now it was a cry to Shasta:

"Run, little brother, run!"

Very Near Eaten by a Bear

It did not need the crying of the Blue Jays to make Shasta run. He was covering the ground almost with the speed of the wolves themselves.

Now he began to slant down towards the timber, darting down the mountain, leaping from boulder to boulder in the manner of the mountain-sheep. Yet behind him, faster and faster, as the rush of his great body gathered force, the Grizzly launched himself downwards, an avalanche of fur!

Shasta knew only too well that, unless something happened, the chase could not go on much longer. It might be a little sooner or a little later, but the Grizzly must have him at the last unless he could reach the trees in time. The trees were his only hope. If he could reach them, he could escape. For among the many things he had learnt of the ways of the forest folk, he had learnt this also: a Grizzly does not climb. And it was in this one thing only that he could outdo his wolf-brothers: he could climb into the trees!

He looked back. The thing was hurling itself nearer—the fearful avalanche of fur!

Now he began to fear that he could not reach the timber in time. The Grizzly was gaining at a terrible pace. And then a thing happened.

Down aslant the mountain-side there came leaping in tremendous bounds the form of a big she-wolf. On it came at a furious speed, every spring of the powerful haunches sending the long grey body forward like an arrow loosed from a bow. And as she came, there rose from deep in her throat a long-drawn howl—the mustering cry of the wolves when the prey is too heavy for one to pull down alone.

The Grizzly saw her coming but could not stop. He was going too fast to turn so as to avoid the first onslaught. With a snarl of fury Nitka sprang.

Her long fangs snatched horribly. There was a gash behind the bear's left ear. He snorted with rage, and tried to pull up. Before he could do so, Nitka had snapped at his flank and leaped away. Then at last, by a supreme effort, the Grizzly pulled himself up, and turned upon his unexpected foe.

[38]

Very Near Eaten by a Bear

By this time Shasta was well within reach of the trees. But some instinct made him suddenly alter his course and turn towards the cave. The Grizzly, seeing this, started again in pursuit of his prey. Once more Nitka leaped, and the long fangs did their deadly work; but this time the bear, turning with remarkable quickness, hurled her off, and did so with such force that Nitka almost lost her balance. A wolf, however, is not easily thrown off its legs, and again Nitka attacked. Each time she sprang, the bear stopped to meet her. Nitka knew full well what she would have to expect if she came within striking distance of those terrible paws and not once did she allow the Grizzly to get his chance to strike. And every time the bear turned, Shasta was making good his escape, farther and farther up the slope. Yet still the bear continued the chase, as if determined, in spite of all Nitka's fierce defence, to have his kill at last.

But he did not reckon upon two enemies at once, and he did not know that a second one, even more to be dreaded than Nitka, would have to be faced before he could seize his prey.

Shasta had almost reached the cave now. He saw the shadowy mouth of it just beyond the clump of bushes where the great cliff broke down.

Yet if the Grizzly should follow him into the cave! At close quarters Nitka would be no match for the Grizzly. Those terrible paws would have the wolf within striking distance, and then, no matter how bravely Nitka fought, she must sooner or later be killed. Yet, just at the moment, the instinct for home was the strongest thing in Shasta's little mind, and so he made blindly for the cave.

As he darted into it, something shot past it in the opposite direction—something that leaped in the air with a noise that would have sounded more like the snarl of a mad dog— if Shasta had ever heard a mad dog—than any voice of wolf!

Far away in the lonely places of the great barren, Shoomoo had caught the long-drawn hunting cry of Nitka, and had answered it on feet that swept the distance like the wind. With every hair on end, with eyes that shone like green fires, with his chops wrinkled to show the gleaming fangs, Shoomoo hurled himself downwards full in the path of the advancing bear.

The Grizzly saw his coming just in time, and raised himself suddenly to give the wolf the blow which would have been his certain death. Swift as a streak of light, Shoomoo swerved as if he actually turned himself in the air. The Grizzly missed his stroke by a hair's breadth. Before he could strike again, both wolves were upon him. They sprang as with one accord, slashing mercilessly; then, in the wolf fashion, leaping away before the enemy could close.

The fight now became a sort of game. As far as mere strength went the Grizzly was far more than a match for the wolves; but their marvellous quickness put him at a disadvantage. Directly he turned to meet the onset of one, the other sprang at him from the opposite direction. They kept circling round him in a ring. It was a ring that flew and snarled and gleamed and bristled; a ring of wild wolf-bodies that seemed never to pause for a single second. Sometimes it widened, sometimes it narrowed, hemming the great bear in; but always it was a live, quivering, flying ring of shadowy bodies and gleaming teeth.

More and more the bear felt that he was no match for his opponents. Hitherto he had had no fear of wolves: he had held them almost in contempt. But these things that leaped and snapped and leaped again seemed scarcely wolves. They were wolfish Furies to which you could not give a name.

Slowly, step by step, he retreated down the slope. He had given up all thought of the strange wolf-cub now. His one idea was to defend himself from these terrible foes, the like of which he had never encountered before. Deep in his grizzly heart he knew that he was being beaten. It was a new feeling, and he did not relish it. Till now he had been monarch of his range, and other animals had respected his undisputed right. Now the tables were being turned, and a couple of wolves larger than he had even seen were driving him steadily back. Yet he would not turn and run. Something in his little pig-like eyes told the wolves that, whatever happened, he would never take safety in flight. That is one of the ideas belonging to a king. When his back is up against a wall, he must fight to the last. And that is exactly what the bear was looking for—something against which he could place his back. To the left, about fifty yards away, a great spur of rock broke from the mountain-side. If he could once reach that, he knew that he could keep his foes at bay. He knew also, that in order to reach it, he would have to fight every yard of the way.

And up above on the slope, a little wild face peered out from the shelter of the rocks, and watched and watched with shining eyes.

THE END OF THE FIGHT

CHAPTER IV

THE END OF THE FIGHT

IT was a running fight that went on as the great grizzly retreated. The one object of the wolves was to keep him on the move. The bear made furious rushes this way and that whenever he thought he had one of his enemies within striking distance. But as sure as ever he attacked one wolf, it leapt clear with marvellous agility, while the other, like a flash of grey lightning, had snatched at his flank and was off before he could turn. Yet in spite of Shoomoo's greater bulk, it was the onset of Nitka which punished the bear most severely. For the time, Nitka was like a thing gone mad. Her eyes blazed like green jewels, her teeth flashed in a grin of rage. The long suppleness that was her body, bent, twisted, turned and doubled on itself, in a series of acrobatic leaps which bewildered her foe, and

[47]

baffled even Shasta's eyes to see how it was
done. She was not fighting for any mere purpose of hatred or revenge; it was not that she,
as Nitka, wanted to conquer the bear. The
thing that was in her, the fierce unutterable
thing that flamed in her eyes and stabbed nak-
edly in her teeth, was her wild, strange love for
the man-cub she had so curiously made her
own. She did not know why she loved him.
How should she, since the Great Spirit of the
Wild had not told her? It was enough that
the Spirit had put the thing into her heart and
made it to remain. Her own wolf-cubs would
come, and would as certainly go out into the
wolf world that is so wide beneath the stars.
But the little man-cub stayed, winter and summer, autumn and spring, only growing larger
very slowly, because it is the habit of men-
cubs and other gods to grow slowly, and you
cannot build them quickly with never so much
rabbit's flesh nor caribou meat, swallowed and
pre-digested, and brought up again as food.
So Nitka waged this desperate battle for the
life of something she held very dear, and in
her blind devotion would have sacrificed even

her own life sooner than that one morsel of Shasta's hairy little body should suffer harm.

With Shoomoo it was different. He had many reasons for fighting, and they were all good ones. First, he fought for Nitka because he loved her, and had mated with her for life. It was that which, when her long hunting cry for help had reached him, had sent him sweeping along the mountain slopes at such a headlong speed. Bound up with that, the man-cub was her own special property, and therefore partly his. He did not understand the man-cub. Shoomoo never pretended to understand. Left to his own instincts he would not have loved the man-cub. But since the thing belonged to Nitka, and was what she loved, therefore it was for him to be good to it whether he would or no. His second reason for fighting was just as good, and was that, naturally, the grizzlies and the wolves are enemies, and have nothing in common except the desire to kill, when the bloodthirst is on them. But there was even a third reason as good as either of the others, and this was that Shoomoo dearly loved a fight. It was not that he was a disagreeable person, always ready to pick a quarrel, for he was anything but that, and quite contented to go his own way peacefully so long as no one disputed it with him. But when a fight was forced upon him, or there was anything to be gained by being fierce, then he wrinkled back his chops in a most threatening manner, and made ready for his deadly spring.

So all these reasons combined made Shoomoo a very dangerous foe, and were the causes which forced the grizzly, who might have coped with Nitka alone, to retreat towards the rock.

It took the bear some time to do this; but once he felt the rock against his back, he reared himself up on his haunches, with his little pig-like eyes red with rage, and towered above the wolves like the giant that he was.

Neither Nitka nor Shoomoo, savage though they might be, were so angry as to be fools. They knew perfectly well that to attack a grizzly in such a position would be the extreme of madness. One blow from one of those terrible steel-tipped paws, striking with the force of a sledge-hammer, and the wolf that met it

would be knocked clean out of the fight. So
they contented themselves with crouching at
a safe distance, and waiting to attack again the
moment the bear should leave the rock. But
if the bear ever had such an idea in his huge
head he thought better of it, and stayed where
he was. And so the time passed, the wolves
not daring to attack the bear, the bear not
daring to quit the protection of the rock. And
it was not until the afternoon had waned into
evening, and the sunset gold had melted behind
the deep forests, that the wolves drew back
towards the den and the grizzly slipped away
into the dusk.

It was many weeks before Shasta recovered
from the effects of his fright and was ready
to carry his explorations any distance from
the cave. And though Nitka did not punish
him, and Shoomoo said nothing, going about
his business silently in the same old way,
Shasta knew quite well that he was in disgrace
and that he had better behave accordingly.
So he contented himself by sitting a good deal
in the doorway of the den and watching the
happenings of the world from that safe posi-

tion. It was not what you would call a very tidy doorway, and there was no mat on which to wipe your paws if you got them muddy with creeping after young geese along the boggy borders of the ponds on the barren. There was a fine litter of feathers, fur and bones, and the little odds and ends of what had once been game. Shasta, squatting humpily in the middle of the mess, looked out with large eyes to snap up the happenings in the world as they fell out through the hours.

Not that very much happened that you could call important. Sometimes a lynx or a fox would steal softly by, sniffing the air suspiciously, and keeping at a safe distance, with sidelong glances at the den. Or sometimes a shadow would appear and disappear between the stems of the pine trees with bewildering swiftness, and a marten would vanish upon his bloodthirsty way. And then, if larger game kept out of sight and smell, there were always the grasshoppers and woodmice chirruping and scurrying in the tall and feathery grass. But after a time Shasta grew tired of this do-nothing life at the door of the den, and began to take little walks here and there, though he kept a sharp look-out, and was always ready to go scampering back to the den at the first hint of danger. And one thing he learnt from his adventure with the grizzly was, always to attend to the warning of the blue jays. Whenever their harsh voices rose from the ordinary gossipy chatter to a warning scream, Shasta would make off at once without waiting to discover what it was that had caused them to sound the alarm.

GOMPOSH, THE WISE ONE

CHAPTER V

GOMPOSH, THE WISE ONE

THE moons went by and the moons went by. The slow moons slipped into each other and were tied into bundles, a summer and a winter to each bundle, and so made up the years.

Shasta did not know anything about that measuring of time, nor that people talked of growing older out there in the world. All he knew was that there were day and night, and that the great lights came and went in the heavens, stepping very slowly upon gold and silver feet. But he knew when the loon, the great northern diver, cried forlornly in the night, that the long cold was at hand, and that he would have to stay in the cave to keep himself from freezing to death. And then it was that Nitka and Shoomoo exerted all their arts to keep the man-cub alive; and when the small

[57]

game grew scarce, and the caribou hunting began, many and many a chunk of venison the little Shasta devoured, and throve marvellously upon the uncooked meat. The meat made him warm, and kept the rich blood at full beat in his veins; and that he might be the warmer when he slept, he scooped a hole in the side of the cave, filling it with dry grass and leaves and a lining of fur and feathers torn from the outside of his meat. He learnt this nest-making from the homes of the wild creatures he discovered in his ramblings in the early spring and summer; for everything you learnt then seemed somehow to be in preparation for the grim time of the winter, when the blizzard howled from the north, and even the wolves, and the caribou they hunted, had to flee before the blast.

It was after many summers and winters had been tied together in bundles that one bright September morning Shasta left the cave and made for a tall rock, overlooking the gorge of the stream. When he reached it, he squatted down and watched what might happen below. No one saw him there—the little brown thing on the rock; and no one minded him, which was even more important, because he perched above the level of the run-ways, and of the creatures whose noses are always asking questions of the lower air.

But some one whom Shasta did not know, and who was wiser than all the other wise folk of the forest, was also out for a walk that wonderful autumn morning, and on soft and padded feet came softly down the mountain slopes above Shasta's airy perch. And this was Gomposh, the old black bear.

Gomposh was very old and of a wonderful blackness. When he walked out in the sun the light upon his fur rippled in silver waves. As for his years, not even Goohooperay, the white owl, could tell you how many they were, much less Gomposh himself.

It was not any sound Gomposh made that told Shasta of his presence, but suddenly, without any warning to his eyes, or ears, or nose, Shasta *knew*. And this was owing to that unexplained sixth sense which the wild animals possess, and which Shasta, after his long dwelling among them, shared to a remarkable degree. He turned round all of a sudden, and there, not fifty feet away, stood Gomposh the Old in all the wonder of his black, black fur.

For the first moment Shasta felt afraid. Here was another bear—smaller, indeed, than the grizzly, but none the less a bear! And now, if the black bear meant mischief, escape was impossible because the rock was too steep for any foothold on the outer face of it, and between its inner side and the open mountain stood the bear. Then, in some odd way which he did not understand, the fear passed, and he knew that this time he was in no danger at all, and that the newcomer with the black robe would do him no harm.

Gomposh waited for a while, observing Shasta with his little wise eyes and making notes of him inside his big wise head. Then, very deliberately and slowly, he came down the slope towards Shasta and sat down on his haunches before him on the rock. For a minute or two neither of them spoke, except in that secret language of eye and nose which makes unnecessary so much of the jabber that we humans call speech. But presently Shasta

[60]

VERY DELIBERATELY AND SLOWLY, HE CAME DOWN THE SLOPE
TOWARDS SHASTA AND SAT DOWN ON HIS HAUNCHES

began to ask questions in wolf-language and
Gomposh made answers in the same. And the
sense of what they said was as follows, though
the actual words were not our human words
at all, but deeper and sweeter in the meaning
of them, and much nearer to the truth.

"Shall we be brothers, you and I?" Shasta
asked, a little timidly, for he was feeling shy.

Gomposh looked at him kindly out of his
little pig-like eyes.

"We *are* brothers," he said. "I am old
Gomposh, brother to all the forest folk."

"*I* am brother to the wolves," Shasta replied.

"You will find yourself brother to many
strange folk before you are much older,"
Gomposh said, and when he had finished he
gave a slow wag with his head.

"Who are the folk?" Shasta asked wonder-
ingly.

"Ah!" Gomposh said, looking even wiser
than before. He looked so tremendously full
of knowledge that Shasta felt very small and
ignorant indeed.

"There are the lynxes and the foxes to begin with," Gomposh said after a pause. But Shasta shook his head.

"No," he said. "They are not brothers. We have no kinship with them, we of the wolves."

Gomposh looked at him for a minute or two without speaking, and Shasta felt uncomfortable.

"It is not for you to say who are not brothers," Gomposh said gravely. "You are not a wolf!"

Shasta blinked his eyes at that. It was the first time any one had told him that he was not a wolf.

"But I am!" he said. "Nitka and Shoomoo and the brothers—we are all of the wolf blood. I have many brothers," he added, as if to make the matter clearer. "They are all out in the world."

"I am aware of that," Gomposh said; "but many brothers do not make you different from what you are."

Shasta could not think of an answer to that, so he was silent for a little time, while something which began to be a question grew big within his head.

"If I am not a wolf, what am I?" he asked at last.

"You will find that out later on," Gomposh said with aggravating calmness. "At present it is enough for you to know what you are not."

"But I don't know it," Shasta said bravely, because he was not going to give way weakly before a bear, if he were never so old, and never so wise. "How do you know that I am not a wolf?"

Gomposh blinked and did not answer for a moment or two. He was taken by surprise, and was just a little shocked. In all his long experience, reaching over many years, no one had ever questioned his wisdom before, nor asked him how he knew. The man-cub was very impudent. It would have been the easiest thing in the world, with one cuff of his big black paw, to teach the man-cub manners, and send him spinning from the rock. But although Gomposh had a great idea of his own

importance, he had also a kind heart, and there
was something in him which went out tenderly
towards the little naked cub, impudent though
he was. So he contented himself with being
very stiff and stand-offish when he spoke again.

"I have eyes," he said. "I have also a nose.
You are not wolf to my eyes, and you are only
half wolf to my nose."

This was a knock-down blow to Shasta, and
he didn't know what to say.

"I am sorry if I don't smell nice," he said
lamely after a while.

"I didn't remark that you didn't smell
nice," Gomposh said. "Smell is a thing for
everybody to decide on for himself.

"What is the smell in me that isn't wolf?"
Shasta asked.

"That you will know later," Gomposh replied.

"But when?" Shasta asked. "Today, or
tomorrow, or when the moon is full?"

"That I do not tell you," Gomposh said.
"When the time comes, you will know."

And that was all Shasta could get out of
him. Gomposh either couldn't or wouldn't

say more, and when he had sat for a little while longer he got up and slowly walked away.

Shasta watched him disappear into the chaparral thicket to the left, and heard him for some time afterwards as he knocked the rotten logs to pieces in his search for grubs.

For a long, long while Shasta sat where he was and gazed down the gorge. An odd feeling that was almost unhappiness was in his head and his stomach, and the feeling went rolling over and over inside him and knocking itself against the corners of his brain. "Not a wolf! Not a wolf!" the feeling kept rapping out. Then, if he was not a wolf, what was he? he asked himself. His memory, groping backwards into the dim beginnings of his life, worked hard to uncover the secret of what he really was; but, try as he would, he could remember nothing but the den and the wolf life that had its centre there, and the happenings of the mountain and of the forest, and the ways of their folk.

There was nothing else—no shapes of tall beings that carried bows in their fore-paws

[65]

and walked always on their hind legs—nothing that told him of his Indian birth.

The morning slipped into the afternoon, and still Shasta sat motionless, humped upon the rock. His eyes were down the gorge, or on the opposite ridge where the tops of the spruces were jagged against the sky. Down below him, on the old run-ways that had threaded the thickets since the beginning of the world, the creatures came and went. Shasta knew them each by sight. He had known them all his life. Yet now, as their familiar forms came noiselessly like shadows over the grass, he had a peculiar feeling of being separated from them by the new knowledge that, somehow, he was of another world. When the thin smell of the twilight came drifting through the trees, then, and not till then, Shasta slipped down noiselessly from his rock and stole homewards to the den.

But in the dark the odd feeling was still questioning: "If I am not a wolf, what am I?"

SHASTA SINGS THE WOLF CHORUS

CHAPTER VI

I'T was one night not long after his conversation with Gomposh that Nitka made it plain to Shasta that he was to accompany her and Shoomoo for some unknown purpose. Shasta had grown used to the appearing and disappearing of foster-brothers every year, and so the four half-grown wolves that trotted by his side on the eventful night were quite familiar to him, and did not perplex him in the least.

It was a very clear night, with the stars shining down through the tall tops of the pines and a faint glimmer low down in the northeast where presently the moon would lift her mighty bowl of silver and water the world with light. Now and then a little waft of wind would send a shiver through the trees, and when it died away the stillness of the

[69]

forest was deeper than before. It was very dark under the trees. Unless you had Indian's or wolf's eyes you would not have been able to see your hand in front of your face. But the eyes that were in Shasta's head were Indian with a wolf's training, and were almost equal to the wolves'. He saw many things which no child born of white people has ever seen since America was discovered nor ever will as long as the world shall last, because the dwellers in the forest are very wise and wary and are a part of the Great Secret that is hidden amongst the trees; and many of them are never seen at all except by the wild animals themselves, and you will not find their names in any work on zoology (which is the polite word for Natural History), because zoology, after all, is only the science which divides things into classes according to their teeth.

Yet although Shasta's eyesight was nearly as keen as the wolves', his speed was not as fast as theirs, and so the going was slower than it would have been if the pack had been alone. For all that, Shasta's pace was only slow compared with the wolves, and if you had seen him running on all fours you would have thought that his speed was very quick indeed.

The order of their going was in this manner: Shoomoo went first (as became the leader of the pack); after him, in single file, came two of the cubs; Shasta followed next, with a wolf brother on each side of him, but slightly behind, so as to guard him if any danger threatened; last of all, with her keen eyes glowing like coals, came old Nitka, bringing up the rear. It would have been a fearless animal indeed which would have attacked such a pack travelling in this wary way. Even a grizzly, or a bull caribou, would have thought twice before encountering the combined force, and would have wisely turned aside without disputing right of way.

Where they were going—what it all meant —Shasta could not guess. He had never travelled at night like this before. The most he had done after dark was to go short distances from the cave and back again, and that never alone, but always with either Nitka or Shoomoo somewhere close at hand. But this long journey was unlike anything he had ever done before. It was strangely exciting: it made the blood dance in his veins. He felt that something big was going to happen, and that now at last he would learn the secret of the wolves. For although he had lived the life of a wolf all these years, there was a feeling in his heart that there was something else, something he had yet to learn, before he should be one with the wolves, as of their very blood. And the feeling, reaching upward from his heart, tugged at his brain with tiny fingers that groped always in the dark.

After some time they left the trees behind them and came out upon the open mountain. Then it was a long climb upwards, going aslant the mountainside towards the east. There was more light now, for the time of moonrise was close at hand. Shasta could see the vast shoulder of the mountain hump itself up against the stars. That was ahead. Behind, and to the right, the canyon plunged down into a hollow of darkness that seemed bottomless. His ears caught the sound of a

[72]

dull roar. He knew it would be a stream beating against the boulders and complaining huskily as it went. The going was faster now, for the land was open, and Shasta increased his pace. Soon they reached a bench, or terrace, along the side of a gorge. Running lightly along this, Shasta heard another sound. It was long and mournful, sliding up and down a minor scale of unutterable grief. It came drifting over the mountains as if the wind carried it, dropping it at times, and then taking hold of it again. Though it was so faint it was not like the voice of a single wolf, but of many wolves singing in chorus together by the silver edges of the moon. He expected his companions to stop and answer it. He had often heard them sing that same song at moonrise, or just before dawn, but, to his surprise, the pack swept on as if they had never heard that sorrowful voice sobbing along the air.

The terrace came to an end abruptly in a spur of rock, but Shoomoo, with a great bound, leaped to a higher ledge and the pack followed. Shasta could not leap in the wolf manner. He climbed instead, using his feet and hands with wonderful agility.

The upper ledge brought them to the summit of the mountain. Here a wide caribou barren stretched away in an unbroken extent to the north and east. There was good hunting here, as the wolves knew. Many and many a fat caribou cow might be cut out of the herd and pulled down when the right season came, but they were not for hunting now. Something quite as strong as the hunting cry was calling to them, and they would obey it in spite of everything else.

On the summit of the mountain the cry Shasta had heard before came again. Only this time it was loud and clear, filling all the spaces of the night with echoes that sounded hollowly from far away. And now Shasta was aware that the wolves were not alone. Other dusky forms were flitting silently on ahead, and to the right and left. As they went on the number of these shadowy forms increased. They were all going in the same direction, and evidently with the same purpose, whatever that might be.

[74]

Shasta Sings the Wolf Chorus

Soon Shasta saw the great rocks rise up ahead. They had passed over the summit of the mountain now, and were descending the brow. The rocks, jagged and torn into all sorts of peculiar shapes, formed a fringe to the downward slope. Beyond, the country fell away sheer to the prairies below. As Shasta approached the rocks he saw that they were alive. On all their ledges and pinnacles wolves were crowded. There were many hundreds of them. He could not have believed that there were so many wolves in all the world! And they were all howling together in a wild, uncanny chorus that, to Shasta's ears, was like a swinging song, very beautiful to hear. Only it was terrible also, and sent shivers down his back. And his heart beat wildly, and he felt as if he had not eaten food for many days.

He could not tell how or why, but suddenly he found himself sitting upon a rock, surrounded by the wolves. And then, as he watched them with their heads thrown back, and their long noses pointed to the stars, he felt something which he could not understand taking hold of him. He could see the wolves plainly now, for the moon was rising. She was behind the mountain yet, but the light of her coming was abroad in the sky.

Shasta looked round to see if Nitka or Shoomoo was close to him. At first he could not distinguish them among the number of the other wolves. Then he caught sight of the great bulk of Shoomoo at the summit of a rock, cut out blackly, like granite, against the rising of the moon. There were many other big wolves there, for it was a gathering of all the packs, but none was as mighty as Shoomoo, towering there, like a king, upon his rock. Once he had found Shoomoo he did not search for Nitka or the foster-brothers. He was simply content to know that they were there. It was upon Shoomoo that his eyes were fixed, for he felt dimly as if, somehow or other, he was the centre of the mystery and the wild heart of the song. And then, immediately behind Shoomoo's giant form, a disc of silver showed suddenly, and the first gleam of the moon-rising shone down upon the wolves.

The singing had been wild before, but now

in the moonlight it grew wilder still. It was enough to make even an Indian's flesh creep to hear this uncanny chorus from hundreds of wolfish throats, rising and falling in the stillness of the night. And for miles and miles, through the endless spruce forests, down the black-throated canyons, along the dreary barrens of the caribou, the wild song went sobbing in a passion of despair. Not an animal, winged or four-footed, in all that savage region but was awake and shivering to the sobbing of the wolves. Kennebec, the mighty eagle, caught it, dreaming far away upon his midnight crags. Gomposh, the old wise one, heard it, sitting in the mouth of his cave on the blue pine hill; and, as he listened, he rumbled a reply—a low, deep growl that seemed to roll about inside him and never got farther than his chest. And far away over the prairies, on the lonely ridges where the Indians bury their dead, the coyotes caught the chorus and, howling dismally, flung it back. Now and then, on the outskirts of the wolf-ring, a fox would appear from nowhere, sit down on his tail, and lift his snout and sing. For though,

[77]

in the usual course of things, the wolves and foxes are sworn enemies, on the nights when the great chorus is sung the foxes are allowed to give themselves to music, and have no cause to fear.

But it was not alone the creatures of the wild who responded to the cry. Far down at the foot of the mountain where the country of the plains began, Shasta heard an answering chorus in the pauses when the wolves seemed to listen for the echoes of their song. And the chorus, too, was wolfish and utterly despairing, as if the prairie wolves were gathering down below. Yet, though Shasta did not know it, the answer was not a wolf one, but belonged to the Indian huskies, those gaunt starved creatures, part wolf, part dog, which the Indians have bred for long years, and of which the camps are full.

In every pause between the challenge of the wolves, the answer of the huskies was still wilder and fuller of despair. As the moon rose, and the light became stronger, Shasta could see more and more plainly what was going on down there at the mountain's foot.

[78]

He saw peculiar pointed things different from anything he had ever seen before. They were arranged in a circle round something which was very red and bright. He did not know, because there was nobody to tell him, that this bright red thing was an Indian camp fire, and that the pointed things about it were the wigwams of the braves. Beyond the wigwams he could see a row of dark objects. These were the huskies sitting on their tails, and sobbing out their sorrow to the wolves. Sometimes the row would break and the huskies would rush wildly about, yelping and snapping at each other as if they had suddenly gone mad. And then they would gather together again, and sit in a long row, and lift their sorrow to the moon.

Presently Shasta saw something else. He saw forms leave the wigwams and come out into the circle between them and the fire. They were like wolves, but seemed to be clothed with loose skins that covered their bodies and fore-legs. The thing which he noticed most particularly was that they did not go on all fours in the true wolf fashion, but walked upon their hind legs only, with their bodies straight in the air. As far as he could tell, they had come out of the wigwams to listen to the wolves. Yet they made no sound, and continued to listen silently, not letting any voice which might be in them wail forth into the night.

The sight of these dumb creatures on their hind legs made Shasta strangely restless. He wanted to lift his arms and loose his heart out in a cry. And as he watched the figures, the feeling grew. He could not tell—poor little wild soul that he was—that these odd and silent forms were those of his own people; that he belonged to them in his blood and in his brain; and that here, in the wolf-world, he was an outcast from his kin. And the Indians, gazing up at those black wolf-shapes cut out against the stars, little guessed that, among that dusky throng, crouched one of their own tribe, kidnapped long ago by an enemy and left in the forest to die of starvation or be torn in pieces by the beasts.

There was a long pause, broken by neither wolves nor huskies. The silence was so deep that you could almost *hear* the shadows as they shortened under the moon.

All at once Shasta threw back his head and howled. It was the true wolf howl, long, vibrating, desolate. The desire to do so came on him suddenly, unexpectedly; a thing wholly strange and not to be explained. The note sang out sharply into the air. It seemed to rip, like a wolf's fangs, the silver throat of the moon.

The wolves cocked their ears and listened intently. Here was a new voice which they had never heard before; a wolf voice truly, yet with some fine difference which set it apart from all others and made it impossible to forget.

When Shasta had ended, and the last dim echo of his howl had faded from the rocks, he sat silent, shivering with fear. For now he had done what only a leader of a pack had the right to do—he had broken in upon the silence of the wolves.

What would they do? Would they punish him for his impertinence? Suppose some leader gave the signal for the entire pack to sweep down upon him and tear him limb from limb? Nitka and the foster-brothers would not be strong enough to save him. Even Shoomoo's giant bulk would be of no avail against the fury of the united pack. Always before when he had known fear, he had taken to his legs, and either he had escaped to the cave in time or else Nitka or Shoomoo had been at hand to save him; but he knew that his legs would be useless now. The great fear seemed to take from them the power of running, and to freeze him to the rock.

He did not move a muscle. He did not even dare to turn his eyes. Yet he saw everything with astonishing clearness down to the smallest detail. There was Shoomoo, motionless on his pinnacle, his ears erect, his hair bristling, the moonlight falling silverly on his dark coat and casting his shadow blackly down below. And there were the countless members of that vast pack equally motionless, equally alert, all their heads turned in one direction, all their gleaming eyes turned one way. And Shasta, seeing all those terrible eyes fixed upon him, not only saw them, but felt them—felt the fierce wolfish thought behind that united all the pack into one wolf-mind.

The silence was terrible. No arrow-headed flight of wild geese came honking from the north to break it. Not even the solitary song of the white-throated sparrow on his fir branch slipped softly out to show that he was awake and that there was a sweetness in the night; and if nothing sounded, so also nothing stirred, nothing except the wolfish shadows that shortened invisibly under the moon.

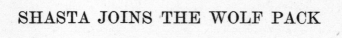

SHASTA JOINS THE WOLF PACK

CHAPTER VII

IN that terrible silence when Shasta trembled with the fear that was in him, and did not dare to move, the great thing happened.

The stillness of the wolves, which was in itself so horrible a thing, as if the whole pack was only waiting for some signal to hurl itself upon him—began to show signs of breaking up. Here and there a head would wag, and a lolling tongue show between white fangs. A she-wolf would snap at her neighbour. A half-grown cub would lick his chops, growling softly in his throat. A stir, a restless movement, set the pack heaving. Teeth were bared and hackles rose. A thousand eyes glimmered in the shadows of the moon. The restlessness increased, growing moment by moment. The pack swayed, bristled, became one wolf-throat

[87]

with a growl like the rumble of an avalanche.

There came a supreme moment before the pack began its dreadful work. If nothing happened before the moment passed, then Shasta would be doomed. It was then that the thing happened and that Shasta breathed again.

Like an arrow from the bow, like the avalanche itself, with a roar like a mountain lion, the giant Shoomoo loosed himself from his rock! Down he came, over the heads of the startled wolves, with a leap that made the eyes blink. He brought himself up suddenly, right over Shasta's body. The boy made no attempt at resistance, and was knocked down by the blow.

But even in that instant, while his head struck the rock, and he felt a stab of pain, he knew that Shoomoo would not hurt him, that underneath Shoomoo's protection he would be safe.

He lay flat on his back, with the big wolf's body above him, blotting out the night. A sweet feeling of warmth and tenderness ran

in his blood. Some sure thing whispered at
his heart that Shoomoo would tear the pack
to pieces, or be himself torn, before he would
allow it to touch a hair of the little body that
lay so confidingly there.

The astonished wolves gazed at this extraordinary thing. At first it looked as if Shoomoo
had given the signal to attack, and, to the
younger wolves, it seemed as if the moment of
the kill had arrived. These half-grown wolves
surged forward, leaping over the backs of the
older wolves, who, with more wisdom, hesitated, gazing warily at Shoomoo. But these
rash younger ones, in the face of Shoomoo's
bared fangs, realized their mistake before it
was too late and drew back. One, however,
paid the penalty of his rashness. He was a
trifle duller-witted than the others. He failed
to catch, as they did, that swift message from
mind to mind, which, among the forest creatures, is like an electric current, warning them,
in the tenth part of a second, what to seek and
what to shun. Even as they rushed forward
the other wolves had caught the message, and

had held themselves back just in the nick of time. The duller cub had blundered, and he had blundered to his fate.

Snarling with rage, Shoomoo met him in his leap, and with one slash of his fangs, ripped his throat. Then, breaking his neck, he flung him clean over his shoulders down the precipice behind.

After that, not a single wolf dared to approach. The renown of Shoomoo's powers as a fighter had spread through the wolf-world far and wide. It was by reason of this that he was not known merely as one of the great pack leaders, but held a position which made him a sort of king over the combined packs.

And now it was plain, even to the dullest, that Shoomoo had taken the man-cub under his special care. If Shoomoo befriended the man-cub any wolf who dared to dispute his right must run the risk of death. Moreover, what was even more important, Shoomoo's claiming Shasta as his, proved beyond any argument that, henceforward, Shasta would have to be regarded as a member of the pack.

The wolves, old and young, wise and foolish, looked on at this astonishing thing, said nothing, and licked their chops.

When Shoomoo had satisfied himself that the pack had learnt its lesson and that Shasta's life was in danger no longer, he moved aside, lifting his large paws delicately, so that he should not touch the child. And then Shasta sat up, a little dazed because of the blow he had received, and rubbed the sore place on his head, and smiled at the wolves.

And when Shoomoo, walking very deliberately and stiff-legged, his tail arched with pride, moved toward his rock, Shasta went with him, and took up his position at his foster-father's side.

When they were seated together on the rock Shoomoo threw up his long snout, and sent a deep howl shuddering to the moon. Shasta took it up, and sent his own voice spinning after it. Then, as with one voice, the whole pack replied. And then again that wild wolf-chorus rose and fell, chanting, sobbing, wailing its unearthly dirge out into the silent hollows of the night.

And down below, the tall shapes of the Indians went back to their tepees, where sleep came to them, in spite of the "medicine" of the wolves, because sleep is the greater medicine.

When the last wailing sob had died away, and the last lonely echo came shivering from the peaks, the wolves began to go. There was no signal for a general move. They went singly, or in little companies. Shasta, looking down from his rock, saw the pack thinning by slow degrees. As a single wolf, or several, departed, they seemed to detach themselves from the edges of the pack softly, as vapours do from the blown edges of a cloud. And these vapour-like forms drifted across the open ground without any sound till they were lost along the barren, or in the shadow of the trees. Soon, out of all that vast pack, not fifty wolves were left. Then there were only twenty-five. At last there remained but Shoomoo, Nitka, the foster-brothers and Shasta himself.

The moon was still high overhead, intensely bright and the shadows of the rocks had a marvellous blackness. The vast and solemn woods hung like folded nightmares, along the mountainsides. The silence seemed like a solid thing which you could strike with a stone and set humming.

Shasta, breathing deeply after his howling song, looked down curiously on the Indian village far below. The bright redness in the middle of it still glowed, but less brightly than before because the fire was dying. All round it the tepees stood in a motionless ring. Shasta did not know that they were tepees, nor even that they were not alive. They seemed to be waiting there and listening. Now that the wolf-chorus was over he half expected them to move. No sound came up from the huskies, which, like the wolves, had disappeared. They had slunk back to the tepees and were now fast asleep. No sound; no movement. Shasta wondered what it all could mean, and where those strange wolves were hidden that could go upright on their hind feet. It was a mystery which his little brain could not solve. He wanted to ask Shoomoo, but something seemed to tell him that it would be useless, and that Shoomoo would not be able to explain.

Presently Shoomoo stretched himself, laid back his ears, and yawned. Then he leaped down from the rock and trotted off. Shasta followed at once, because he knew that the moment Shoomoo went the rest of the family would move, and he had no wish to be left alone in that unearthly place which seemed to lie somewhere between the gorges and the moon.

They went back in the same order as they had come—Shoomoo leading, Shasta in the middle, Nitka bringing up the rear. Down the mountain slopes, along the ravines, through the endless leagues of forest, they passed in silence like a procession of grey ghosts. It was the same trail also. Never for a yard's space did they quit that long back trail. And they were the same wolves, not altered in the least degree from what they were before. Yet to Shasta all was different in an odd way which he did not understand. He seemed to be closer to his wolf kindred

than ever before—to have a finer sense for all
they did and were.   Up to the present he had
lived with them, played with them, eaten and
slept with them; but now he seemed to be one
with them as he had never been before.   And
this, though he did not know it, was because
of the singing of the wolf-chorus; because he
had sung himself, as it were, into the very
heart of the Wild.

THE VOICE THAT WAS GOOHOOP-
ERAY

CHAPTER VIII

THE VOICE THAT WAS GOOHOOPERAY

TWO days after the chorus night Shasta was out for a prowl by himself. The prowling instinct was strong within him now. He loved to creep into the forest alone and climb a tree above some run-way to see who was abroad. The deer drifted past like dreams, lifting their feet delicately and wrinkling their noses upwind; or a fox would sneak along, ears, eyes, and nose on the alert, but never seeing Shasta above him on his perch. And sometimes the wolves would come, two or three in single file, and Shasta would make cub noises at them, and take a huge delight in watching their astonishment as they looked up into the trees.

On this particular night he had not perched long in his chosen tree when he heard the dreary wail of Goohooperay come sobbing

down the dusk. Shasta only knew Goohooperay as a voice, a dark unhappy voice that
wailed along the twilight and climbed up and
down the night. Goohooperay's body lived
in a hollow hemlock, and slept there all the
day. It was a brown body and downy withal,
and beautiful with fat sleep. But when the
sun had set behind the Bargloosh, and the
gloaming was beginning to gloam, then Goohooperay squeezed his body out of the hemlock, and the fun began.

It began by his sitting just outside his front
door and ruffling his feathers and stretching
his great wings. That was to get the sleep out
of him and think what a nice bird he was and
set his wits to work. And when everything
was in proper working order he opened his
hooded head and loosed out his voice; and
then it was that, near and far away, the forest
people gave heed to the whooping cry and
answered in their hearts. Those who had
been asleep in the thickets during the drowsy
afternoon stretched themselves and yawned.
The cry seemed to say "Good hunting!" and
that now they must bestir themselves and get

abroad. To some it boded well, and would mean a fat kill; but to others ill, and being killed themselves, for Goohooperay himself was a killer, and very far from being a vegetarian. But that is the way with owls; it is not a pleasant way or a sugary way. If you are an owl, you do owlishly; and Goohooperay was very much an owl.

When he had sent his voice far along the dusky trails Goohooperay would spread his wings and go sailing after his voice. And as he glided through the tops of the spruces, or went swooping down the gorge, he did not make the faintest sound to tell you he was there; only a great winged shape would come slanting through the tree and—*swoop!*—some rat or leveret would wish it hadn't been there!

It was some time before Shasta learnt that Goohooperay had a body as well as a voice. Often and often when that melancholy sound went drearily past, Shasta would shiver with something that was almost fear, and would wait for it to come again. And sometimes other voices would answer Goohooperay's, and the echoes would be mocking in the hollow gorges, but always there was something peculiar about his, which set it apart from the others, so that you could recognize it again.

Goohooperay was feeling particularly cheerful this evening, and whenever he felt like that he always put an extra miserable wobble into his voice. It was very misleading of him, though he didn't mean to deceive. As a matter of fact, he was a most contented soul, and had never had an unhappy night in his life. As for the "Hump" or the "Dump" or anything silly like that, Goohooperay would have *sobbed* with amusement if you had suggested anything of the sort. But he loved pretending to be sad. To sit on a dead limb and hoot and hoot, till his heart seemed to be breaking, gave him an exquisite delight.

When Shasta heard the long, haunting cry which he had heard so often before, he had a sudden desire to find out if there was a body which sat behind the voice. So, without any hesitation, he slid down from his tree and travelled towards the sound. Twice before he reached the hemlock Goohooperay wailed his melancholy pleasure-note, and unwittingly guided Shasta to the spot.

At first Shasta could not see plainly what manner of person Goohooperay might be, for the shade of the hemlock was very black, and Goohooperay's front door was well within it. But when Shasta stole up to the very foot of the tree and gazed up into the enormous eyes above him, he realized that the voice had, indeed, a body behind it.

For a long time the bird and the boy observed each other in silence. Goohooperay felt that it wasn't his place to begin a conversation, and Shasta didn't like to; but at last he plucked up courage and began. But the beginning, the middle, and the end of his conversation were only odd little wolf-noises that he gurgled in his throat. They were not in the least like words, but that didn't matter, for behind each gurgle there was a thought which, by some secret means which human folks couldn't understand, spilled itself out of Shasta's head into Goohooperay's, and made the meaning plain.

It would be impossible to tell exactly what they said to each other in the shadow of the hemlock, for owl language is not translatable like Arabic or Greek. If it were, there would be a Brown Owl Grammar and a Brown Owl spelling-book, and some other pieces of monstrous literature which we are mercifully spared. For the Brown Owl's library is not bound in calf—though you can sometimes catch the flutter of its leaves in the flowing of the air—and the letterpress of the twilight is too dim for human eyes.

Suddenly Goohooperay's great yellow eyes stopped gazing at Shasta, and glanced outwards into the dusk. There was such an intense and solemn look in them that Shasta looked, too. Just beyond the shade of the tree he thought he saw something that went slowly past, but he couldn't be sure. It had no shape. It was as if a piece of the twilight had broken adrift from the rest. A little waft of air accompanied it with a whispering sound. Then, whatever it was, it had gone by, and everything was as before.

Shasta was startled. He turned quickly to

[104]

Goohooperay and asked him what it was. But
Goohooperay only swelled out his feathers
hugely, and was dumb. Then he hooted his
long cry, listened intently to catch the effect,
and, spreading his wings, floated away.

And that was how Shasta learnt that Goohooperay was a body as well as a voice, and
how he saw, for the first time in his life, the
passing of the Spirit of the Wild. For, indeed, that Spirit is little spoken of in these our
times, and I think seldom seen, for our eyes
are not accustomed to the old beautiful shadows that are for ever going by. It is only the
animals who see them, or those who walk continually in the great spaces or have their dwelling within sound of the trees.

THE COMING OF KENNEBEC

CHAPTER IX

THE wolf-brothers were playing in the sun. There were four little brown cubs, very fat and puppy-like, and full of fun. They chased each other up and down, and had wrestling matches and biting competitions, and all sorts of rough-and-tumble games. Shasta sat in the mouth of the cave watching them and laughing softly to himself. He had known many a lot of wolf-brothers, and they were always the same funny, fat, frolicsome little rascals until they grew too old to frolic, and began to get their fighting fangs and be ready for the fierce work of the grown-up world. Shasta loved all his foster-brothers and never forgot them, even after they had gone out into the world. And not a single wolf-brother ever forgot *him,* or would have refused to fight for him to the

[109]

death if he were in danger. Every year
Shasta looked forward to the appearing of the
fresh lot of cubs, and loved them with all his
heart as soon as they were born. Only he had
an instinct which warned him that when they
were very new babies they were not to be
touched; for although Nitka remained devoted
to her man-cub, she would not allow him to
meddle with the babies while they were very
new, and partly out of respect for her wishes,
and partly for fear of what she might do if
he disobeyed, Shasta never touched a cub until it was a moon old; while Nitka, though she
would never allow anything to approach the
cave—not even Shoomoo himself—while the
cubs were small, would let Shasta come in and
go out as he chose, so long as he kept to his
own end of the cave and did not interfere with
her while she mothered the new family.

This morning she had gone down to the
stream to drink, and lie awhile by the run-
way to see what might come by. She only
intended to be a short time away, and had left
Shasta on guard while she was gone. Shasta
liked to feel that Nitka trusted him, and that

he was doing an important thing. It was a very warm morning, and everything seemed at peace. A sweet, clean air blew along the trails, and those who used them scented it delicately and went springily, because of the pent-up life that was in them, and the goodness of the world.

High up on the opposite ridge a lynx was sunning herself and her kittens outside her den. With her keen eyes she swept the landscape near and distant in a glance that noted everything and lost nothing. Though Shasta could not see *her,* she saw *him* and the cubs perfectly. She was no friend of the wolves, as they knew full well, but this morning the historic enmity between them seemed to lie low, and she stared at the little group calmly with no blazing hate in her green eyes.

A big red fox came down to the edge of the lake. He stood with one forefoot up, all ears and nose, scenting and listening for any hint that should come from the trail; and, as he listened he wrinkled his nose, wobbling it quaintly to catch whatever faint smell might come drifting his way.

In the shallows the buffalo-fish were basking on the bottom with the water flowing softly over their gills, and the sunlight shining on their scales. Up in the high blue a pair of fish-hawks sailed airily on the look-out for food. But the buffalo-fish were so busy doing nothing that they escaped observation. They guessed the hawks were somewhere about, but they just lay low and didn't say a word; and it is surprising how much mischief may be avoided simply by doing nothing! Old Gom-posh was having a good rub against his favour-ite tree. It was plastered with mud and hair, and was quite as plain to read as a book, if you only knew how to read the "rub." He set his back against the rough bark, and rubbed and rubbed till the most exquisite sensations went thrilling down his spine.

But all these quiet little happenings were really of no consequence to the wolves. What *did* matter was—although they didn't know it—that, high up on the tall crags, Kennebec, the great eagle, was thinking wickedly.

When Kennebec thought wickedly some one was sure to suffer. He would sit on the

[112]

pointed summit of a crag, which was now worn
smooth with the constant gripping of his great
claws, and his wonderful eyes would shine with
a strong light. Down below him, for a thousand feet, the tops of the spruces made the forest look like a green carpet worn into holes.
And beyond that, to the south, the lake glimmered and shone, and the Sakuska showed in
loops of silver. Over the lake Kennebec could
see the fish-hawks at their fishing. He looked
at them in his lordly way, watching them, ready
to swoop at the first sign of a fish. He could
not catch fish himself, but that made no difference to his diet. When he felt like fish, he
waited till one of the hawks swooped and rose
with a fish in its claws. Then Kennebec
would sail out majestically from his crag and
bully the hawk till it dropped his prey. Before the fish touched the water Kennebec, falling in a dizzy rush, would seize it in his talons
and bear it off in triumph. But this morning
he was for bigger game, and the glare that
came and went in his eyes was a danger-light
to any who should be so unfortunate as to see
it. About fifty yards to the left of where

he sat a cleft rock held his nest. It was a huge mass of sticks, filling the cleft from side to side. In the middle of it two young eaglets sat and *gawped* for food. Their mother would bring it to them presently. Kennebec was not in a mood to worry about that! They could gawp and gawp till she came! And if they thought their gawping would have any effect upon him, they might gawp their silly heads off without upsetting *him!*

Suddenly he lifted his great wings, loosed the pinnacle with his horny feet, and plunged into space.

Below him the world seemed scooped out into a vast abyss. He rose higher and higher till he was nothing but a speck in the surrounding blue.

.   .   .   .   .   .

Shasta, watching the foster-brothers lazily, saw the speck appear in the high blue. At first it was no larger than a fly. Then it grew and grew till it was the size of a grasshopper, then of a fish-hawk. And then the blue jays began to scold.

Shasta had never forgotten the lesson of the

blue jays. When they scolded he knew that something was happening, and that you had better watch out. He looked quickly about him on every side, throwing the keen glance of his piercing eyes down into the forest and up among the rocks. So far as he could see, nothing stirred. If any enemy was approaching, it was coming unseen, unheard, along the mossy ways. Yet there was no sign of any living creature upon the Bargloosh, nor in all the wide world beside, except that solitary fish-hawk circling overhead.

Yet, although he couldn't see anything, Shasta had a sort of feeling that he ought to drive the cubs back into the den. They would be safe there whether anything happened or whether it didn't. And the blue jays went on scolding all the time. But surely Nitka must hear them and know what was going on! If she didn't take the warning and come racing back, then it was because nothing *was* going to happen.

Moment after moment went by, and still she lid not appear. Shasta was growing more and more uneasy. In spite of not seeing anything, there was a vague feeling that something was wrong. That strange warning which comes to the wild creatures, no man can tell how, came to him now. The screaming of the blue jays had aroused him, but the warning had come independently of them. It was so clear, so unmistakable, that he made a wolf-noise in his throat to attract the attention of the cubs. Then suddenly he was aware of something overhead.

He looked up quickly. The fish-hawk had disappeared. Instead, a winged thunderbolt was dropping out of the sky. It fell from a dizzy height with a rush so swift that it seemed as if it must dash itself to pieces on the earth before it could stop.

Shasta was spellbound. He could not stir. Then, before he had time to understand, the thunderbolt had spread wide wings, and Kennebec was hovering overhead.

Shasta heard the rustle of those tremendous wings, and a swift fear shot into his heart. But his courage did not forsake him, and, with a howl, he sprang to protect the cubs.

It was too late. Before he could reach them

The Coming of Kennebec

Kennebec had swooped, and, when he rose again, he bore a wolf-cub in his claws.

Just as he did so, however, and while he was still beating his wings for the ascent, a few feet from the ground, Nitka, her hair on end with fury, came leaping up the slope.

As she reached the spot she made a mighty bound in the air, springing at the eagle with a snarl. But Kennebec was already under way. Nitka's bared fangs clicked together six inches short of his tail, and she fell back to the earth with a moan of grief and rage.

Shasta, looking on, felt his body shivering like a maple leaf in the wind. He was terrified of what Nitka might do in the present state of her mind. As Kennebec, flying heavily, passed slowly over the tree-tops in his gradual ascent, the she-wolf's eyeballs, riveted upon him, blazed with fury. As long as he remained in sight, growing gradually smaller in the distance, she raged up and down, with the saliva dropping from her jaws. She had been roused by the screaming of the jays, and had come racing back as soon as she realized that something was wrong. But she was too late to prevent the tragedy. And now the horrible thing had happened, and she would never see her cub again!

As soon as her straining eyes could no longer follow the flight of the robber, she hustled the other cubs back into the cave. But that was all. She did not turn on Shasta, nor even so much as growl at him as he sat shivering in the sun. He waited miserably at the mouth of the cave, wondering if Nitka would come out and comfort him; but she remained inside for the rest of the afternoon, trying to console herself for her loss by fondling the three remaining cubs. And after a while Shasta crept away to his look-out above the valley, where he had met Gomposh for the first time.

He had not been there very long before he heard a sound of rustling and tearing to the left. Then the great form of Gomposh himself pushed itself into the glare of the golden afternoon. He had been refreshing himself in his clumsy way among the wild raspberry bushes, and as he came out was licking the juice from his mouth. He came along slowly, his little eyes glancing right and left for any sign of food. There was a hollow log lying full in his path. He gave it a heavy blow with his paw, and then put his ear close to listen to the insects in its crevices which he had disturbed. Evidently what he had heard satisfied him, for he ripped open the log with one slash of his paw, and then proceeded to lick up the grubs and scurrying insects. When he had finished, he caught sight of Shasta and came lumbering towards him.

As before, they sat together on the rock, and said nothing in a very wise way. But presently Shasta unladed himself of his heavy heart, and told Gomposh all his grief.

And old Gomposh wagged his head slowly, and let Shasta understand that that was only what had happened many, many times before in his memory, and was likely to happen as many times again. Eagles would be eagles, he said, as long as feathers were feathers and fur was fur. And if wolf-cubs would also be fat and juicy and lollop in the sun, then what were you to expect if Kennebec came by, and admired the fat rolls at the back of their absurd little necks?

[119]

But besides that, he gave Shasta to understand that Kennebec was worse than other eagles, and had worked more destruction in his time than any other person with wings.

Shasta's talk with Gomposh was a very long one, for the thoughts that were in them oozed out slowly, and trickled drop by drop into each other's minds. Yet though the dripping was slow, the thoughts were clear as crystal, and plain to understand. That is the difference between animals' talk and ours. The beasts speak seldom and with perfect understanding; while we humans stir up our thick brains with a stick that we call an idea, and pour out floods of muddy talk!

At sunset Gomposh lumbered back into the woods, and Shasta took himself home. He crept very softly into the den, because he felt that he was in disgrace. But Nitka was off hunting and the cubs were fast asleep.

Very early in the morning Shasta stole out again. He went along swiftly, following a caribou trail that trended south. It was one of the old forest trails which had been used for centuries by the journeying caribou in their autumn and spring migrations. He went on steadily, following the directions which Gomposh had given him the evening before. Gomposh knew all the trails of the forest; where they came from and where they led to; also what sort of company you were likely to meet on the way.

Shasta met but few travellers in that pale time just before dawn, and of those he met he had no fear. One was a big timber wolf travelling slowly after a kill. His eyes flashed when he saw Shasta; but Shasta spoke to him in the wolf language, and in a moment they were friends. And although Shasta did not recognize the wolf, the wolf remembered Shasta, for he was one of those who had taken part in the great wolf chorus on the memorable night.

Then, when they had spoken a little and rubbed noses together, to show that they were members of the wolf family, they parted, each going on his separate way.

It was late that evening before Shasta reached the end of his journey. It was a place monstrously tall, and everything there

[121]

shot up to an immense growth as if it had been sucked upwards by the white lips of the moon in the tremendous nights. Right before him a precipice glimmered vast, and built itself up and up towards the stars.

He lost no time, but curled himself up at the foot and fell asleep; and all night long his dreams were of Kennebec, whose eyrie was at the top.

With dawn he was up, and began to climb. Though the precipice looked one huge unbroken wall, it had many crannies and crevices where you might get a foothold if you knew how to climb; and that is just what Shasta could do beyond everything else. He could climb a tree like a marten, and among the rocks his foothold was as sure as that of a mountain sheep.

He went up and up steadily; sometimes he had to wait while he searched for a sure foothold in the gigantic wall. Here and there a shrub or tree would grow out of a crevice, and with the aid of these he pulled himself up, hand over hand, while half his body hung in

[122]

air; and then the muscles of his back stood out like whipcord and rippled along his arms.

As he climbed, the depth under him deepened. He had long passed above the summits of the loftiest pines. Now the forest was far below him, and he was hanging between earth and sky in the middle air. He was climbing from the wolf-world, with its old familiar trails, to the world of the eagles, where the earth trails cease for ever in the trackless wastes of air. What had Shoomoo or Nitka, or the wolf-brothers, to do with this upper world where, surely, if you went on climbing, you must come at last to the sheep-walks of the stars where the pastures are steep about the moon?

And the world yawned under!

A false footing, or the breaking of a shrub, and down he would go to certain death and be dashed to pieces. Yet, in spite of the awful spaces about him and that yawning gulf below, there was no fear in him, nor any dizziness when he looked down. As he rested for a moment, and let his eyes wander, he gazed

down five hundred feet as calmly as if he sat
by the side of a quiet pool and watched the
mirrored world.

If Kennebec had known what was approaching his eyrie on the impossible crags, he would
have launched himself out at the intruder with
fury and dashed him down the precipice; but
he and his mate were far away, having left
before dawn for a long journey, and had not
come back. Up in the nest in the cloven rock,
the eaglets sat and wondered why neither of
their parents returned with food.

After a while Shasta could see the eyrie rock
and the ends of sticks which stuck out from
the side. It was above him—right over the
edge of the precipice. He had just reached
it and was holding on to the branch of a stunted
spruce which grew below the rock, when the
branch cracked. Without it the foothold was
not sufficient, his feet were only clinging to
the roughness of the rock; and suddenly that
great chasm below seemed to suck him back.

For one brief moment fear clutched at
Shasta's heart, and he seemed to feel himself

falling—falling down the steep face of the
world. Then the muscles of his feet braced
themselves, clinging to the rock; before they
relaxed, his whole body became a steel spring,
and, when the branch broke, his arms were
round the stem of the tree. Once his hands
found firm hold there was no more danger;
even with half his body hanging in air it was a
simple thing for him to lift himself into the
tree. In a few moments more he had scaled
the rock and was looking down into the eagle's
nest.

As soon as his eyes fell on the eaglets his
fingers began to twitch. They were horrible-
looking things, scraggy in their bodies and
covered with dark down, with short, stubby
quills sticking out here and there.

Shasta hated these quillish young monsters
with all his heart. They gawped up at him in
their ridiculous way with their beaks open.
The thing he wanted to do was to grab them
at once by their ugly necks and send them spinning down the precipice; yet they looked so
stupid, squatting there, that it seemed a silly

thing to do. If they could have fought, and there could have been a struggle, he would not have hesitated.

The nest was surrounded by a litter of bones and odds and ends of feathers and fur. If the eaglets were hungry it was not for want of gorging themselves in the past; the whole place spoke of Kennebec's ravages, and his constant desire to kill. Much of the food was only half-eaten, showing that there was no need for all this slaughter. It was left there to rot in the sun and to poison the sweet air.

Shasta was still hesitating what to do, when his eye fell on something which set his blood throbbing. It was the remains of the wolf-cub which Kennebec had carried off.

At the sight of it Shasta became a different being; there was wolfish rage in his brain and a strange wolfish glitter in his eyes. He saw, in the ugly forms of the eaglets before him, the hateful offspring of the hated Kennebec, the destroyer of his wolf-brother and the enemy of his race.

The note of anguish in Nitka's voice when she beheld her cub carried away before her

WHAT WAS THAT DRIVING FURIOUSLY UP THE LONG STEEPS OF
THE DAWN?

eyes had not haunted his ears in vain. A
wild desire to avenge his wolf-kindred swept
over him; and now the chance to do so lay
within his power—a chance which, in the
countless moons that followed, might never
come again!

The thing was big; it was tremendous. If
the eaglets were destroyed it would strike at
the heart of Kennebec—nay, at the heart of
the whole eagle world!

Shasta stooped. He seized an eaglet fiercely
by the neck, lifted it, swung it, sent it spinning dizzily out into the void. He watched
it fall, tumbling over and over, down the immense depth, and then strike the summits of
the trees. The second followed the fate of
the first. Shasta looked down savagely upon
an empty nest.

But what was that driving furiously up the
long steeps of the dawn? It was coming
swiftly, terribly, a blazing fire in its yellow
eyes; and as the great wings thrashed the air
the whistling roar of the approach filled all
the hollow space.

Shasta needed only to look once to realize

what was upon him; and that now, if ever, he was face to face with death.

Kennebec had *seen!* *He was coming back!*

HOW SHASTA HID IN TIME

CHAPTER X

HOW SHASTA HID IN TIME

THAT fierce approach of Kennebec, sweeping up as from the remote ends of the hollow world, was a terrible thing to see. Also, when the sound of it reached Shasta's ears, it was terrible to hear. He knew that there was only one thing to do, and that he must do it without an instant's delay—to find some hiding-place where he would be safe from those awful claws and beak; for Kennebec's anger would have no bounds when he discovered that the eaglets had been destroyed.

To descend the cliff as he had come up would be impossible for Shasta, as he was fully aware. Once exposed upon that naked face of rock, Kennebec would attack him with fury, and, ripping him from his foothold, dash him down below. He took in his surroundings with a

[131]

swift glance. The place was composed entirely of rocks. They were jagged and splintered by the frosts and tempests of a million years. They wore a fierce and hungry look, like Kennebec himself. It was the raw edge of the world.

Shasta lost not a moment. He fled along the tumbled rocks, as the mountain sheep flee when they are pursued by wolves. He could not tell where he was going nor where the rocks would end. The instinct in him was to seek refuge among the trees. Surely upon the other side of the precipice he would find that the forest climbed! The forest was his friend, if he could reach it in time. Under the shelter of the spruces he would be safe. The great eagle could not reach him there.

But as he fled he heard the whistling rush of those fearful wings. They were close behind him now—closer and closer! He did not dare to look. He heard; he felt: that was enough.

Now the storming wings were over him. Beating the air Kennebec hovered, waiting for the swift downward rush, which, if it reached Shasta, would be the end. For the moment the air seemed darkened with the shadow of those wings! Then Kennebec swooped. But even as he did so Shasta darted suddenly to the left. He had seen an opening between the rocks, and, with the quickness which only wild animals possess, had bolted in.

By the tenth part of a second and the tenth part of an inch Kennebec missed his aim. Instead of the soft body of Shasta, those terrible claws of his met the hard rock.

For an hour or more he hovered, raging over the spot where Shasta had disappeared. But if he hoped that the boy would come out, he was disappointed. Shasta might be half-wolf in his mind, but that did not make him a fool. On the contrary, his wolf-like instincts taught him to stay where he was, and to lie low as long as that winged fury raged overhead.

The place into which he had crept was little more than a crevice between two enormous rocks, and could certainly not be called a cave. But, narrow as it was, there was ample room for Shasta's little body; and settling himself into as comfortable a position as possible, he was presently asleep. That was part of his wolf-wisdom, learnt he didn't know how: "When there's nothing else to be done, sleep!"

After a time Kennebec grew tired of hovering over the crevice, so he settled down on a near pinnacle to watch. Noon came and went. A burning heat scorched the rocks. It would have been far cooler up in the high levels of the air. Nevertheless Kennebec chose to sit stewing on his rock, with the glare of his great eyes fixed on the spot where Shasta had disappeared. And the glare had a fierce intensity which seemed as if it were fiercer than even the sun's. For the hard and cruel light in it meant death to whatever should come within Kennebec's power to kill.

Late in the afternoon Shasta woke, and peeped out to see if there were any signs of Kennebec. But the pinnacle upon which the eagle had taken up his watch was just out of sight, and Shasta could not see him. In spite of the shade it was very stuffy in the crevice, and the thirst began to dry Shasta's tongue. He thought of the cool green trails of the forest, and water sliding under the moss with a hollow trickle. Now that Kennebec seemed to have gone, it was a great temptation to slip out and make a bolt for the nearest trees. Although they were not in sight, he was sure they must be there, just over the other side of the rocks. Yet, in spite of the temptation, something told him that it was not safe to go. He could not see Kennebec, it is true, yet a feeling—the sense that seldom fails to warn the wild creatures when danger is at hand— told him to remain where he was. And this obedience to his instinct saved his life. For though Kennebec was out of sight, he was not gone. There he sat, on the burning rock, sultry with heat, but even sultrier with anger, watching and watching with the patience that is born of hate.

It was not until the dusk fell, and the tawny light of sunset faded from the peaks, that he rose from his perch and flapped heavily away.

When it was quite dark Shasta crept out from his hiding-place and made his way softly over the rocks. He went slowly, setting his feet with the utmost care, for he knew that the least sound might betray his presence, and bring Kennebec's terrible talons upon him, even in the dark. At last, to his joy, he saw the summits of the spruces glowing against the stars, and in a few minutes more he was safe beneath the trees.

SHASTA'S RESTLESSNESS AND WHAT CAME OF IT

CHAPTER XI

AFTER Shasta's exploit against Kennebec, he became doubly marked as a person among the forest folk. Along the Wild news flies quickly. It is carried not only by swift feet and keen noses: it seems to travel as well by mysterious carriers, who spread it through the length and breadth of the land. What these carriers are, and what is the manner and meaning of their coming and going, only the wild creatures know. *They* see them with their large eyes which deepen with the dusk! *They* hear the soft whisper of their going on the wind-trails of the air! We should not see them, you or I, because our eyes are too accustomed to the artificial lights, and because around our minds are built the brick walls of the world. But

[139]

the wild creatures, whose eyes have never been dulled by electricity, nor their ears stunned by the roar of the motors, see and hear the spirit faces and the flowing shapes which go by under the trees.

So not many hours had passed before the great news of Shasta's coming had spread through the wilderness. And particularly the wolves took hold of it, and regarded Shasta as a sort of little god. No one had ever dared to dispute Kennebec's mastery before. Kennebec was so high and mighty that whatever he did must be suffered, even though you raged against it in your heart. But now the strange cub had done the unthinkable deed. He had done it and escaped. All those who had lost their young through Kennebec's evil claws rejoiced that now at last the tyrant was punished, and felt their wrongs avenged. Never more would Kennebec feel safe upon his precipice that climbed up to the stars. Feet and hands that had scaled it before might do so again. The fear of it would haunt him through the burning days and the breathless nights.

[140]

Yet, in spite of Shasta's growing importance among his wild kindred, a strange restlessness began to stir within him, and to move along his blood. And when the mood was strongest, his thoughts turned continually towards the place of the rocks where he had joined the wolf chorus and sung himself into the heart of the pack. It was the memory of the music which haunted him most, and when, from afar off, he would hear some wild wolf-note come sobbing through the night, the sound would set him thrilling till every hair on his body seemed to be alive. Yet always, following hard upon the remembrance of the chorus, would come that other memory of tall wolfish shapes, that moved on their hind legs, and of that red glow in the circle of things that did not move: all of it down there, at the foot of the precipice, as if one looked down through the canyon of sleep to the low lair of a dream.

One day when the thing was strong upon him, he met Gomposh, and asked him what it was. Gomposh said little, but thought much. He knew that at certain seasons all things follow a craving within them, and that it made

them follow far trails, leading to distant
ranges from which they did not always return.
The geese went north, honking their mysterious cry. The caribou made long journeys,
and deepened the ancient trails. The mountain sheep left their high pastures, guided by
an instinct, which never failed, to the salt-lick
in the lowlands to the south. And now it was
plain to Gomposh that the strange cub had a
craving within him also. It was not to find
a lair in the north, nor a salt-lick in the south.
It was not to change pasture for pasture, in
the way of the caribou. Gomposh knew certainly that it was none of those things; but that
it was the call of the blood that was in him, the
secret Indian call, that penetrated even
through the deep forests, far into the inmost
heart of the wilderness where he lay outcast
from his kind. But though Gomposh thought
the thing clearly enough in his deep mind, he
did not worry it into actual words.

"It is a good restlessness," he said. "It is
of the other part of you that is not wolf. Follow the restlessness of your blood."

That, in the sense of it, was what Gomposh

gave Shasta to understand, though he said it in his own peculiar way.

After that Shasta's mind was very busy with the new thing that had come to him, and before long he let it have its way, and started on his journey by himself. The wolves watched him go, but did not attempt to stop him. The growing unrest that had been in him had not escaped them. For, apart from the feeling which it produced, Shasta's outward behaviour was different from before. He came and went continually, restless and ill at ease. The very air about the cave seemed to breathe unrest, and the wolves themselves became restless, though they could not tell the reason why. Yet, although they did nothing to hinder him in his final departing, Nitka's eyes watched him regretfully as his little body disappeared among the trees.

He travelled on without stopping until he reached the spot where the great chorus had taken place. As he approached the neighbourhood, he grew more and more excited. The memories of that wonderful singing night came crowding back upon him. It was broad daylight now, for it was at the middle of the afternoon; and when he reached the high rocks, he could see far and wide over the foothills and the prairies beyond. He marvelled at the bigness of the world, and at the vast sunny spaces, shadowless in the heat. Out there in the immense sunlight there were no forests to break the glare. The heat glimmered and swam. It was as if the sunlight were a beating pulse. From where he crouched first the Indian camp was hidden; but his curiosity was too strong to allow him to remain where he was; so, very cautiously, he crept to the extreme edge of the rocks and looked over.

There it was, the same strange circle of things which he could not understand. Also the upright wolves were there, walking about singly, or standing in little groups. Shasta watched them intently with shining eyes. And as he looked, the confused murmur of an Indian camp rose to his ears—voices of men and women, the barking of dogs, and the crying of children; also a slow and measured sound, which seemed to the boy to be even more disquieting than the other unaccustomed noises—

[144]

the beating of an Indian tom-tom for a sacred
dance. He was so intent upon watching the
camp below that it was only a slight noise behind which made him aware that danger was
approaching. He turned his head quickly and
then remained spellbound.

Not a dozen paces away stood a tall form,
motionless as a rock. Its hair was long, falling to its shoulders. A single eagle's feather
stood up straight behind the head. It was
dressed in tanned buckskin, and carried a
bow of sarvis-berry wood. The quiver, from
which the ends of the long feathered arrows
appeared, was of the yellow skin of a buffalo
calf. Shasta gazed at this strange apparition
with awe. Somehow or other, he felt that it
had to do with the camp down below. He was
afraid of it. He wanted to run. Yet an over-
mastering desire to look his fill at the thing
left him where he was. For a minute or two
the Indian and the boy looked at each other
without making a sound. Then the Indian
made a step forward, and Shasta growled low
in his throat.

If Shasta was astonished at the Indian, the

Indian was equally astonished at Shasta. The
boy's appearance was extraordinarily wild.
His matted hair fell straggling over his face.
In order to see clearly, he had to shake it out
of his eyes continually. It was more like an
animal's mane than human hair, and gave him
a ferocious look. His constant exposure to
the sun and air, unprotected by any clothes,
had thickened the short hair upon his body
till it was covered completely with a fine
downy growth.

When the Indian heard the wolfish snarl he
paused. Through the thick mane of Shasta's
head he saw the gleam of intensely black eyes.
Then he advanced again.

Shasta looked sharply to left and right,
measuring distances. Then he leapt to his
feet and began to run. But he ran in wolf
fashion, on all fours. Fast though he went,
the Indian was faster. He heard the quiet
pad of moccasined feet behind him. Terror
seized him. His one thought was to gain the
shelter of the friendly trees. Before he could
reach them, however, the Indian was upon him.
Shasta felt something seize his hair behind.

[146]

His first instinct was that of a wild animal trapped, and he turned in fury upon his assailant. But before he could do any damage, the Indian threw him down, and fastened his arms with a throng. It was in vain that Shasta struggled with all his strength to free himself. The Indian was too powerful and the deerskin throng held fast. When he was finally secured, his captor lifted him under his arm and carried him down towards the camp.

After struggling fiercely for some time, Shasta became still. It was not only that he felt that further resistance would be useless. Something seemed to tell him that, as long as he remained quiet, the Indian would do him no harm. For the first time since he was a tiny papoose, the smell that clings about all things Indian came to his nose. It was an unfamiliar smell, yet, somehow, it was not new. His eyes and his ears had brought with him no memories of his forgotten infancy: his nose was faithful to the past. What faint, glimmering memories of the Indian lodges it brought; of the camp fire, and the cooking;

of the buckskin clothes and untanned hides; all the clinging odours of that old Indian life —who shall say? Now, as he was carried captive to his own people, quite unconscious though he was that he belonged to them, the Indian scent was a pleasant thing, so that he was soothed by it, and even, for the moment, subdued.

It took some time to gain the camp, for the downward way was steep, and there was no trail. Moreover Shasta, lying limp as he did, was a dead weight, and not easy to carry. At last the descent was made, and the camp reached. The Indian put his burden down.

SHASTA SEES HIS REDSKIN KINDRED

CHAPTER XII

NOT more than a couple of minutes had passed before the news of the capture had gone through the camp. The Indians, old and young, men, women and children, came crowding round to see this strange monster which Looking-All-Ways had found. Shasta, sitting hunched upon his calves, glared round at the company with his beady eyes shining through the masses of his hair. The Indians, seeing the glitter of them, thought it wiser not to come too close, and every time Shasta threw back his head to shake the hair out of his eyes, a murmur went through the crowd.

Looking-All-Ways told his tale. He had been hunting on the caribou barren, behind the high rocks. On his return, he had come upon the little monster crouching on the rocks where the wolves had gathered, and looking down upon the camp.

Poor little Shasta gazed at the strange beings around him with wonder and awe. He
did not feel a monster. It was *they* who were
the monsters—these tall, smooth-faced creatures with skins that seemed to be loose, and
not belonging to their bodies at all! No wonder his eyes glittered as he turned them quickly
this way and that, taking in all the details
of his surroundings with marvellous rapidity.
The thing excited him beyond measure. He
felt a growing desire to throw back his head
and howl.

For a time nothing happened. The Indians
were content to stare at him in astonishment,
while Shasta glared back. Then the chief,
Big Eagle, gave orders that his arms should
be untied. Looking-All-Ways stepped forward and unloosened the deer-skin thong.
Shasta submitted quietly, for he had a strong
feeling within him that it was the best thing
to do. Only he wanted to howl so very badly!
Yet he kept the howl down in his throat, and
crouched, humped up, with his hands upon the
ground.

Suddenly one of the Indians, bolder than the

rest, touched Shasta's back, running his hand down his spine. Like a flash, Shasta, whirling round, with a wolfish snarl, seized the offending hand. With a cry of fear and pain the Indian sprang back, snatching his hand away. After that, the Indians gave Shasta more room, for now they had a wholesome dread of his temper. If they had not touched him, Shasta would not have turned on them. But the touch of that strange hand maddened him, and set his pulses throbbing. It was the wild blood in him that rebelled. In common with all really wild creatures, he could not bear to be touched by a human hand. And all his life afterwards he was the same. He never overcame the shrinking from being touched by his fellows.

After a while the Indians began to move off, and soon Shasta was left to himself with only Looking-All-Ways to watch him. For some time Shasta stayed where he was without stirring. He wanted to take in his new surroundings fully, before deciding what to do. The only thing about him that he moved was his head and his eyes. He kept moving his head rapidly this way and that, as some un-familiar sound caught his ear. He observed the shapes of things, and their colour and movements, with a piercing gaze which saw everything and lost nothing. And because he was so true to his wolf training, he sniffed at them hard, to make them more understandable through his nose. It was all so utterly new and unexpected that it was like being popped down into the middle of another world. Next to the Indians themselves, the things that as-tonished him most were their lodges. He watched with a feeling of awe the owners go-ing in and out. Some of the lodges were closed. Over the entrances flaps of buffalo-skin were laced, and no one entered or came out. Shasta had a feeling that behind the laced flaps mysterious things were lurking—he could not tell what. Or perhaps they were the dens where the she-Indians hid their cubs. If so, they were strangely silent and gave no sign of life. Many of the tepees were orna-mented with painted circles and figures of animals and birds that ran round the hides. At the top, under the ends of the lodge-poles,

[154]

the circles represented the sun, moon and
planets. Below, where the tepee was widest
and touched the ground, the circles were what
the Indians call "Dusty Stars," and were imi-
tations of the prairie puff-balls, which, when
you touch them, fall swiftly into dust. The
tepee against which Shasta crouched was
ringed by these dusty stars, but he did not
know what they were meant for. He only saw
in them round daubs of yellow paint. And because he knew nothing about painting, or that
one thing could be laid on another, he thought
that the tepees and their decorations had
grown as they were, like tall mushrooms, bitten
small in their tops by the white teeth of the
moon. But wherever his gaze wandered, it
always returned to Looking-All-Ways, who sat
a few paces away towards the sun, and smoked
a pipe of polished stone. And there was this
peculiarity about Looking-All-Ways, that, although his name suggested a swift and prairie-
wide glance, which made it impossible for one
to take him by surprise, he had a habit of sitting in a sleepy attitude, staring dreamily
straight in front of him, as if he noticed noth-

ing that was going on around. Shasta, of course, did not yet know his name. All he knew was that if Looking-All-Ways had a slow eye, he was extremely swift as to his feet. And as he watched him, he measured distances with his own cunning eyes behind his heavy hair. This distance, and that! So far from the last porcupine quill on Looking-All-Ways' leggings to the nearest toe-nail on Shasta's naked foot! So far again from the toe-nail to the dusty stars at the edge of the tepee; and from the tepee itself to that lump of rising ground toward the northwest! Shasta began to lay his plans cunningly.

If he made straight for the knoll, Looking-All-Ways might catch him before he could reach it, but if he darted behind the tepee, he might be able to dodge and double, and make lightning twists in the air, and so baffle the Indian until he could reach the trees. As always, when in danger, Shasta's instincts turned toward the trees. It was not until long afterwards that he learnt the ancient medicine song and sung:

Shasta Sees His Redskin Kindred

"The trees are my medicine.
When I am among them,
I walk around my own medicine."

Shasta was nervous of the tepee—he did not know what might be immediately behind it. That was one reason which kept him so long where he was. If he could see what was on the other side he would feel better, and more inclined to run. Another reason was the sense of being surrounded on all sides by strange creatures whose behaviour was so utterly unlike the wolves that there was no saying what they would do the moment he started to run. Yet, whenever he looked away from the lodges, there were the high bluffs and the precipices, and the summits of the spruces and the pines, like the ragged edges of the wolf-world. That way lay freedom, and the life that had no terror for him, and in which he was at home.

The more he looked at the tree-tops over the summits of the rising ground to the northwest, the more he felt the desire growing in him to be up and away.

At last the moment came when he could

bear it no longer. He glanced warily at his captor before making the dash. The time seemed favourable. Looking-All-Ways had his eyes upon the remote horizon. There was a dull look in them as if they were glazed with dreams. Suddenly, without the slightest warning, Shasta leapt and disappeared behind the tepee.

The thing was done with the quickness of a wolf. In spite of that, the slumberous-looking mass of the Indian uncoiled itself like a spring. The dream-glaze over his eyeballs vanished in a flash. Instantly they became the eyes of an eagle when he swoops.

Shasta had scarcely reached the back of the tepee when the Indian was on his feet and had started in pursuit. This time Shasta did not make the mistake of running a straight course. He made a zigzag line through the outermost tepees, turning and twisting with bewildering quickness. Even when he darted out into the open, he did not run straight. It was a marvel to see how he turned and doubled. And every time when Looking-All-Ways, with his greater speed, was almost upon him, Shasta would draw his muscles together and leap sideways like a wolf. And every time he leaped, he was nearer to freedom than before.

Suddenly something happened which he could not understand. Looking-All-Ways was not near him. He was farther behind than he had been at the beginning of the chase. Yet Shasta felt something slip over his head, tighten round his body with a terrible grip, and bring him to the ground with a jerk. When he looked round in astonishment and terror, there was his pursuer fifty paces away, at the other end of a raw-hide lariat!

Shasta struggled and tore at the hateful thing which was biting into his naked body. But the thing held. The more he struggled the tighter it became. It was dragging him back to the camp. In a very few minutes he was among the lodges again and knew that escape was hopeless.

After this attempt, the Indians secured him firmly with thongs, one of which was fastened to a stake driven in the ground. They were fond of making pets of wild animals. And now they felt they had in their midst a creature so wonderful that it was more than half human, and which might prove to be a powerful "Medicine" to the tribe. Once more they crowded round the strange boy, and jabbered to each other in their throats. Shasta had never heard such odd sounds. The strange eyes in their hairless faces troubled him, but the noises that came out of their mouths made him tingle all over. It was not until near sunset that the crowd separated, the Indians going back to their evening meal.

Shasta looked wistfully at the sun as it dipped to the mountains, rested for a moment or two upon their summits and then disappeared. The sun was going to his tepee, and the stars which decorated it were not dusty. But they would not bind him with deer-thongs, the people in those lodges; for nothing is bound there, where the sun and moon go upon the ancient trails. And of those trails only the "wolf-trail" is visible, worn across the heavens by the moccasins of the Indian dead.

The smell of the cooking came to Shasta's nose, and tickled it pleasantly. Not far off,

a group of squaws were cooking buffalo
tongues. Seeing his eyes upon them, one of
them took a tongue from the pot and threw
it to him with a laugh. Shasta drew back, eye-
ing it suspiciously—this steaming, smelling
thing which lay upon the ground. But by degrees the pleasant smell of it overcame him,
and he began to eat. It was his first taste of
cooked food. When he had finished, he licked
his lips with satisfaction, and wished for more.
But though the squaws laughed at him, they
did not offer him another, for buffalo tongues
are a delicacy and not to be lightly given away.

The smoke of many fires was now rising
from the lodges. Besides the cooking, Shasta
could smell the sweet smell of burning cottonwood. As the dusk fell and twilight deepened
into night, the lodges shone out more and more
plainly, lit by inside fires. And in the rising
and falling of the flames the painted animals
upon the hides seemed to quiver into life, and
to chase each other continually round the circles of the tepees. Then, one by one, the fires
died down, and the lodges ceased to shine.
They became dark and silent, hiding the sleep-

ers within. Only one here and there would give out a ghostly glimmer like a sentinel who watched.

As long as the lodges glimmered Shasta did not dare to move. He felt as if the dusty stars of them were eyes upon him. But when the last glimmer died, and all the tepees were dark, he began to move stealthily backwards and forwards, tugging at the thongs.

But, try as he would, he could not loosen them. They were too cunningly arranged for his unskilled fingers to undo, and when he tried his strong white teeth upon them he had no better success.

The camp was very still. Presently the wind rose and made the lodge ears flap gently. Shasta did not know what it was, and the sound made him uneasy. All at once there was another sound which set his pulses throbbing.

It was a long, sobbing cry, coming down from the mountains. In the midst of his strange surroundings it was like a voice from home. He knew it for the voice of a wolf-brother walking along the high roof of the

world. He waited for it to come again. In
the pause, nothing broke the stillness, except
the gentle flap, flap of the lodge-ears at the
top of the tepees.

Again the cry came. This time it sounded
less clear, as if the wolf were farther away.
Shasta felt a desperate sense of loneliness.
He was being left to his fate. If the wolf-
brother went away and did not know that he
was there, how would he carry a message to
the rest of the pack? For if Nitka only knew
that he was taken captive by these strange
man-wolves, surely she would come and rescue
him, if any power of rescue lay in her feet
and paws.

Shasta did not wait any longer. He threw
his head backwards and let out a long, howling
cry. It was the genuine wolf-cry. Any wolf
hearing it would recognize it at once, and answer it in his mind even if he did not give
tongue.

The noise aroused the Indian huskies, but
before they yelped a reply the wolf on the
mountains howled again, and Shasta knew
that his call had been answered. He howled

back louder and more desperately than before. The mournful singing note went with a throb and a quiver far into the night, and the wind, catching it, sped it farther on its way. Again the answering cry came back from the mountains. It came singing down the canyon like a live and quivering thing.

Now the huskies could bear it no longer. They broke out into a loud clamour, rushing about wildly, and yelping at the top of their voices. In a moment, the whole camp was astir. The Indians rushed out of their lodges to see what was the matter, shouting to each other and bidding the women and children stay where they were. Looking-All-Ways came running to Shasta, fearing lest he should have escaped. But Shasta, the cause of it all, sat there quietly crouched in front of the tepee, and making no outward sign, though every nerve in his body was tingling with excitement.

It was some time before the camp settled down again and peace was restored. Every now and again a husky would whine uneasily, or give the ghost-bark which Indians say the dogs give when spirits are abroad. But by degrees even these uneasy ones dropped off to sleep, and no sound broke the intense still-ness which brooded over the camp.

Shasta, however, had no thought of sleep. His mind and body were both wide awake. To him the silence was only a cloak, which muffled, but did not kill, all sorts of fine sounds that trembled on the air.

The wind had dropped now, and the flapping of the lodge-ears had ceased. He listened in-tently, waiting, always waiting, for what he knew would come.

It was in the strange hour just before dawn that two grey wolf-shapes came loping down the mountainside. They approached the camp warily, bellies close to the ground, and eyes a-glimmer in the dark.

It was Nitka and Shoomoo.

The huskies were fast asleep and did not hear them. On they came, moving as sound-lessly as the shadows which they seemed.

They crept in among the ring of tepees. On all sides lay the sleeping Indians, uncon-scious that, in their very midst, two great wolves were creeping towards their goal.

If Shasta had been on the leeward side, he would have scented their approach, but he sat crouched to the windward of the wolves and was not aware of their coming until they had actually entered the camp. Then his wolf-sense warned him that something not Indian was moving between the lodges. So that when, suddenly, Nitka's long body glided into view, he was not astonished, and not in the least alarmed. Her cold nose against his arm, and then the warm caress of her tongue, told him all she wanted him to know. Close behind her stood Shoomoo. But he did not caress Shasta. As usual, he kept his feelings to himself, and waited for Nitka to take the lead.

Nitka had never seen deer-thongs before, nor how they could bind you so that you could not move. But her keen brain soon took in the problem, and once her brain grasped the thing she was ready to act. Holding down with one paw the thong which bound Shasta to the stake, she set her gleaming teeth to work. Shoomoo followed her example, and in a very few minutes the thing was cut, and Shasta was once more free.

Directly Shasta felt that he was free, a wild joy took possession of him. It was not the Indians themselves that terrified him so much as the feeling of being a prisoner in their hands. To be bound, to be helpless, not to be able to run when you wished—that was the terrible thing. The creatures themselves— the smooth-faced hind-leg-walking wolves— seemed harmless enough. At least, they had not yet shown any signs of wanting to hurt him. And something almost drew him to them with a drawing which he could not understand. Still, the thing which made it impossible to feel they were really friends was this being bound in their midst, with this horrible raw-hide thong. Directly Nitka's teeth had done the work, and he felt that he could move from the stake, his own thought was to make sure of his freedom by leaving the camp without a moment's delay.

So far, nothing seemed to have warned the Indians what was going on. The camp was wonderfully still. In a few minutes more the dawn would break. When it did, danger would begin for all wild things within or near the circle of the camp. Above, the stars still shone brightly between the slow drift of the clouds. The tall shapes of the lodges loomed black and threatening, like creatures that watched. Now that the work for which they had come was finished, both Nitka and Shoo-moo were uneasy and anxious to be gone. The smells of the camp did not please them as they had pleased Shasta. To their noses, they were the danger scents of something which they did not understand. And *fear* was in their hearts. It was not the fear that wild animals have of each other; it was deeper down. It was the instinctive fear of man.

As soon as she had gnawed through the thong, and nosed at Shasta to satisfy herself that he was not only free but able to make use of his legs, Nitka gave the sign to Shoomoo. What sign it was, no one not born of wolf blood could have told you. Even Shasta could not have done so, though he was aware that the sign was given, for the unspoken sign-language of the animals is not to be cramped into the narrow shapes of human speech. Whatever the sign was, Shoomoo obeyed. He slid round the nearest tepee as noiselessly as if his great body floated on the air. Shasta followed, with Nitka close behind. She had led the way into the camp, because of her greater cunning, but now it was for Shoomoo to find the way out. Her place now was close to her strange cub, so that she could protect him on the instant from any danger that might threaten.

Two grey shadows had drifted into camp. Now *three* were stealing out, under the stars, and no human eye watched their stealthy departure. All would have been well, if an unlucky husky dog had not happened to wake as the three shadows glided past.

There was a short bark, a rush, and a worrying snarl. Then one piercing yelp rent the silence, and the husky lay a bleeding form, thrown by Shoomoo's jaws three yards away. With that the whole husky pack was on its feet, roused from its slumbers in an instant. At least twenty furious dogs hurled themselves at the wolves. Never had Nitka and Shoomoo

a finer chance to show their fighting power.
From two large grey timber-wolves they
seemed to transform themselves into leaping
whirlwinds that snatched and tore, and flung
husky dogs like chaff into the air. At first
Shasta was in the centre of the fight. He
could not, of course, help his foster parents,
for his teeth and hands were useless at such
a time; all he could do was to save himself as
much as possible from the brunt of the attack.
This he did by crouching, leaping and running
when the right moment came. Beyond everything else, he kept his throat protected with
his arms, for his wolf-knowledge and training
taught him that this was the danger spot,
which if you did not guard, meant the losing
of your life.

Once or twice he felt a stinging pain, as a
husky snatched at him and the sharp teeth
scored his flesh; but each time the dog paid
dearly for his rashness, and was not for biting
any more. It was only when Nitka or Shoomoo was busy finishing a dog that the thing
happened. Otherwise, they kept close to
Shasta, one on each side, guarding him from

[170]

attack. Each time Shasta was touched, Nitka's anger passed all bounds. She not only punished the offender with death, but she tore at the other dogs with redoubled fury.

So the fight rolled towards the forest—a yapping, snarling mass of leaping bodies and snatching teeth. In its track the bodies of dead and dying huskies lay bleeding on the dark ground.

The thing that Shasta dreaded most was lest the Indians should come to the rescue of their dogs. But having had one false alarm, they did not trouble to rouse themselves again, and even Looking-All-Ways remained on his bed of buffalo robes and said evil things of the huskies for disturbing his repose.

It was not many minutes before the fight was over. The huskies, finding themselves outmatched by the superior strength and fury of the wolves, began to lose heart. When the moment came that they had had enough of it, the wolves seemed to know it by instinct. They passed in a flash, from defence to attack, and, covering Shasta's retreat towards the trees, they charged the pack with unequalled fury. Such an onset was irresistible. The huskies gave way before it, completely routed. Their only care was how to save their skins, as they fled, yelping into the night. Of the twenty dogs which had attacked the wolves, only ten found their way back to camp; and of these many had ugly wounds which they carried as scars to the end of their days. It had been so great a fight that the Indians marvelled when the morning light showed them the blood-stained ground and the bodies of the dogs that had died in the fray.

All the way back through the dark woods Shasta felt a great joy within him. And the gloom seemed alive with things that gave him greeting as he ran. He could not see them clearly—those things. Yet now and then something shadowy stirred, and swayed towards him, or drifted softly by. And though they were so faint and shadowy, he knew them for the good, secret things of the forest, which none but the wild creatures know. His wounds were a little sore, but, even as he ran, Nitka found time to doctor them with her tongue. She paid no heed to her own. There

would be time enough to attend to them when
they had reached the den. Neither she nor
Shoomoo had really dangerous wounds, although they were bleeding in many places. A
day or two's rest and licking would make them
all right, and as long as their man-cub was
safe they did not care.

It was bright morning before they reached
the den. The sun had risen and was pouring
down upon the Bargloosh all the freshness
of his early beams. From the tip of a fir
branch, a clear little song slipped into the
morning air. It was Killooleet, the white-
throated sparrow, trilling his morning tune.
He had his nest somewhere near the den, only
the wolves never found out where. All they
knew him by was his song, and the flicker of
his flight as he darted daintily past. The very
fanning of his wings seemed to sweeten the
air. As for his song—he spilt it out at them
in little trickling tunes all through the day, or
whenever he happened to wake up in the night.
The old wolves didn't mind him much, one
way or the other, but Shasta was fond of him,
and used to make a gurgle in his throat when-

ever Killooleet spilt his voice. And now, as he approached the cave, the song of Killooleet seemed a welcome home, and when he looked up into the tree there was Killooleet perched on the fir-tip, with the sunlight shining full on his little wobbling throat!

THE BULL MOOSE

CHAPTER XIII

THE BULL MOOSE

GOMPOSH'S lair was in the black heart of the cedar swamp. Old though the cedars were, Gomposh had the feeling of being even older. He liked the ancientness of the place; its dankness and darkness, and, above all, its silence—the silence of green decaying things. It was so silent that he could almost *hear* himself thinking, and his thoughts seemed to make more noise even than his great padded feet. Under the grey twisted trunks, the ground oozed with moisture, which fed the pits of black water that never went dry even in the summer drought. Whatever life stirred in those black pits, occasionally disturbing their stagnant surfaces with oily ripples, it did not greatly affect Gomposh. He preferred not to bother about them, and to devote his mind instead to the clumps of fat fungus—white, red, pink and

orange—which glowed like dull lamps in the
heart of the gloom. The taste of their flabby
fatness pleased his palate. It was not exactly
an exciting form of food; but it grew on your
doorstep, so to speak, and saved a lot of trouble. And when you wanted to vary your diet,
there were the skunk cabbages and other damp
vegetables.

Another thing that recommended the place
to the old bear was its comparative freedom
from other animals. Goohooperay, it is true,
inhabited the hollow hemlock on the farther
side of the swamp, but he seldom came near
Gomposh's lair, since his activities took him
generally to the open slopes of the Bargloosh
where the hunting was fair to medium, and
sometimes even good. His voice, of course,
was a thing to be regretted, and when, on first
getting out of bed, he would perch at the top
of his tree and send the loudest parts of himself shrilling lamentably far out into the twilight, Gomposh's little eyes would shine with
disapproval, and he would make remarks to
himself deep down in his throat. But a voice
cannot be cuffed into silence, when it has wings

that carry it out of the reach of your paw,
and so Gomposh had to content himself with
a little wholesome grumbling which, after all,
kept him from becoming all fungus and fat,
and made him change his feeding-ground from
place to place. The only other bird that ever
intruded upon his privacy was the nuthatch.
But as this little bird, being one of the quiet-
est of all the feathered folk, spent its time
mainly in sliding up and down the cedar trunks
like a shadow without feet, only now and then
giving forth a tiny faint note in long silences,
as if it were apologizing to itself for being
there at all—Gomposh couldn't find it in his
heart to lodge a complaint. He would lie in
his lair for hours and hours, listening con-
tentedly to the fat, oozy silence, and observing
the solemn gloom in which the colours of the
red and orange toadstools seemed loud enough
to make a noise, and wish that the nuthatch
needn't go on apologizing.

The lair was in a deep hollow, between the
humpy roots of a large old cedar. It was dry
enough, except when the rains were very
heavy, as it was tunnelled out on the edge of

one of the Hardwood knolls which rose up
from the swamp here and there, like the last
remaining hill-tops of a drowned world. To
make this hole still more rainproof, and at
the same time warmer, Gomposh had covered
the cedar roots with boughs which he had con-
trived cunningly into a roof! Oh, he was a
wise, wary old person, was Gomposh! and the
experience of unnumbered winters had taught
him that when the blizzards come swirling over
the Bargloosh from the northeast, it is a grand
and comforting thing to have a good roof over
you, thatched thick and warm with snow. So
to this deep cave in the roots of the cedar
when the wind moaned in the draughty tops
of the spruce woods and the frost bit with
invisible teeth, Gomposh, bulging with berries
and fat, would retire for the winter, and sleep,
and sleep, and sleep!

Toadstools and various sorts of berries made
up the principal part of his diet; but as berries
did not grow in the swamp, and after a time
he had eaten all the best toadstools in the neighbourhood of his den, he occasionally found it
pleasant to leave the swamp and ascend to the

blueberry barrens high up on the slopes of the Bargloosh.

One morning, not many days after Shasta's return to his wolf kin, Gomposh got up with the berry feeling in him very bad. It was a little early for blueberries, but there were other things he might find—perhaps an Indian pear with its sweet though tasteless fruit, ripened early in some sunny spot. And anyhow there were always confiding beetles under stones, and whole families of insects that live in rotten logs.

He left his lair, picking his way carefully between the humpy roots that made the ground lift itself into such strange shapes, and setting his great padded feet on the thick moss as delicately as a fox, so that, in case some mouse or water-rat should be out of its hole, he might catch it unawares with one of the lightning movements of his immense paw. At the edge of the swamp he pushed his way stealthily through a thicket of Indian willows and then paused to sniff the air with that old sensitive nose of his which brought him tidings of the trails as to what was abroad, with a fine certainty that could not err. But, sniff as he would, nothing came to his questing nostrils except the smell that was as old as the centuries—the raw, keen sweetness of the wet spruce and fir forests, mixed with the homely scent of the cedar swamp. Yet in spite of this, he did not move without the utmost caution, and, for all his apparent clumsiness, his vast furry bulk seemed to drift in among the spruces with the quietness of smoke.

Far away on the other side of the lake, a great bull moose was making his way angrily through the woods, looking for the cow he had heard calling to him at dawn, and thrashing the bushes with his mighty antlers as a challenge to any one who should be rash enough to dispute his title of Lord of the Wilderness. But as he was travelling up-wind, and was, moreover, too far away for the sound of his temper to carry, Gomposh's unerring nose did not receive the warning as he ascended the Bargloosh with the berry want in his inside.

He was half-way up the mountain, when, all at once, he stopped, and swung his nose into the wind. Something was abroad now—

something with a warmer, thicker scent than the sharp tang of the spruces. What was it? There was a smell of wolf in it, and yet again something which was not wolf. It was a mixture of scents so finely jumbled together that only a nose like Gomposh's could have disentangled them. In spite of his immense knowledge of the thousand ways in which the wilderness kindreds spill themselves upon the air, the old bear was puzzled. So, in order to give his mind perfect leisure to attend to his nose, Gomposh sank back on his haunches, and then sat bolt upright with his paws hanging idly in the air.

The scent came more and more plainly. And as it grew, Gomposh's brain worked faster and faster. The smell was half strange and half familiar. Where had he smelt it before? And then, suddenly, he *knew*.

Shasta, stealing through the spruces as noiselessly as any of the wild brotherhood, thought he had done an extremely clever thing. He fully believed he had caught an old black bear unawares, sitting up on the trail and sniffing at nothing, with his paws dangling

foolishly before him. It was not until the
boy was close upon him that Gomposh quickly
turned his head, and pretended to be surprised.
Shasta, recognizing his old friend, came slowly
forward with shining eyes.

At first Gomposh did not speak, but that was
not surprising. Gomposh was not one to rush
into speech when you could express so much
by saying nothing. To be able to express a
good deal, and yet not to put it into the shape
of words—to say things with your whole body
and mind without making noises with your
mouth and throat—is a wonderful faculty.
Few people know anything about it; because
half the business of people's lives is carried on
in the mouth, and they are not happy or wise
enough to be quiet; but the beasts use it continually; because they are very happy and
very wise.

So Gomposh looked at Shasta, and Shasta
looked at Gomposh, and for a long time neither
of them made a sound. But the mind that was
in Gomposh's big body, and the body that was
outside Gomposh's big mind, went on quietly
making all sorts of observations which Shasta

[184]

easily understood. So he knew, just as well as if Gomposh had said it, that the bear was telling him he had been on his travels; also that things were different in him; that he was another sort of person, because many things had happened to him in the meantime. Exactly what those things were, Gomposh did not know; but he knew what the effect was which they had produced in Shasta. He knew that the part of Shasta that was not wolf had mingled with that part of the world which also is not wolf, and that therefore he was a little less wolfish than before.

At first Shasta felt a little uncomfortable at the way Gomposh looked him calmly through and through. It was as if Gomposh said: "We are a long way off, little Brother. We have travelled far apart. But I catch you with the mind."

And Shasta couldn't help feeling as if he had done something of which he was ashamed. He had left the wild kindred—the wolf-father, the wolf-mother, all that swift, stealthy, fierce wolf-world that had its going among the trees. He had gone out to search for another kindred, almost as swift, stealthy and fierce as the wolves themselves, yet of a strange, unnamable cunning, and of a smell stranger still. And yet with all this strangeness, the new kindred had fastened itself upon him with a hold which Shasta could not shake off, as of something which his half-wolf nature could neither resist nor deny. And the more Gomposh looked at him out of his little piercing eyes, the more keenly he felt that the old bear was realizing this hold upon him of the new kindred, far off beyond the trees.

When at last Gomposh spoke—that is, when he allowed the wisdom that was in him to ooze out in bear language—what he remarked amounted to this:

"You have found the new kindred. You have learnt the new knowledge. You are less wolf than you were."

Shasta did not like being told that he had grown less a wolf. It was just as if Gomposh had accused him of having lost something which was not to be recovered.

"I am just the same as I was," he replied stoutly; but he knew it was not true.

[186]

"The moons have gone by, and the moons have gone by," Gomposh said. "The runways have been filled with folk. But you have not come along them. You have not watched them. You have missed everything that has gone by."

Shasta made it clear that one could not be everywhere at the same time, and that, anyhow, he had not missed the moons.

"No one misses the moons," Gomposh remarked gravely, "except those of us who go to sleep. It is a pleasant sleep in the winter when we go sleeping through the moons."

"Nitka and Shoomoo do not sleep," Shasta said boastfully. "*We* do not sleep the winter sleep—we of the wolves!"

"And so you do not find the world beautifully new when you wake up in the spring," Gomposh said.

That was a fresh idea to Shasta. He knew what a wonderful thing it was to find the world new every day, but it must seem terribly new indeed to you after the winter sleep. The thought of hunger came to his rescue.

face with a big bull moose he nearly jumped out of himself with astonishment.

It was not the first time that he had seen moose. In the early summer, down in the alder thicket at the edge of the lake, Shasta, watching motionless between the leaves, had seen a big cow and her lanky calf come down into the lake. The cow began to busy herself by pulling water-lily roots, and the calf nosed along the bank in an inquisitive manner as if it still found the world a most bewildering place. They did not seem animals to be frightened at; and even the big cow looked a harmless sort of being whose mind, what there was of it, was in her mouth and ears. But the huge bull now in front of Shasta was a very different sort of beast. From the ground to the ridge of the immense fore shoulders, he measured a good six feet. That great humped ridge covered with thick black hair seemed to mound itself over some enormous strength which lay solid and compact ready to hurl itself forth at an instant's notice in one terrifying blow which would smash any object that dared to challenge it. But what impressed

[190]

Shasta more than anything else was the great spread of polished antlers on each side of his head. Antlers like those he had never seen. It was like wearing a forest on your forehead: it made you uncomfortable to look at: it was like being an animal and a tree at the same time.

The moose was equally surprised at Shasta. With all the creatures of the forest—lynxes, catamounts, raccoons, wolves, deer, foxes, bears and chipmunks—he was familiar. But this smooth, hornless, round-headed thing was like none of them. It had a shape and a character extraordinarily different; and the big moose was not pleased. There was another thing that he did not like, and that was Shasta's smell. Not that this was so unfamiliar as his shape. Indeed, something like it the moose had often smelt before. Moreover, it was a smell that always made him angry. It was that of the wolves. And yet, mingled with it in a curious and bewildering way, there was another odour, not so pungent as the wolf scent, but hardly less objectionable to the moose, and that was the smell of man.

[191]

and the Bargloosh was as empty of wolves as the sky of clouds.

At the second cry, the moose stopped thrashing the bushes, and stood still. But along his neck and shoulders the coarse black hair rose threateningly. A red light burned dangerously in his eyes. Suddenly, without warning, he sprang. Quick as a wolf, Shasta leaped aside. If he had been the fraction of a second later he would have been trampled to death. The murderous hoof of the moose missed its mark by a quarter of an inch. Snorting with rage, he raised himself on his hind legs to strike again.

And then the wonderful thing happened. Even as the moose rose, a huge black form hurled itself through the air, descending upon him like a thunderbolt. Before he could deliver the blow intended for Shasta, even before he could change his position in order to protect himself, a huge paw, armed with claws like curved daggers, had ripped his shoulder half-way to the bone.

So great was the force of the blow, with the

whole weight of Gomposh's body behind it, that the moose was hurled to the ground. He had hardly touched it, however, before he was on his feet, quivering with pain and fury. Seeing that his assailant was one of the hated bears, his fury redoubled. In spite of his wounds, now streaming with blood, he rushed savagely at the bear, striking again with his hoofs. But Gomposh, though now old, was no novice at boxing. He simply gathered his great hind quarters under him and sat well back upon them, with his forepaws lifted. Each time the moose struck, Gomposh parried the blow with a lightning sweep of his gigantic paw; and each time the paw swept, the moose bled afresh. Only once did he do Gomposh any injury, and that was when, with a sudden charge of his left-hand antler, he caught the bear in the ribs. But he paid dearly for the action. Gomposh, though nearly losing his balance, brought his right paw down with such sledge-hammer force on his opponent's shoulder, that the moose staggered, and almost fell. The blow was so tremendous that the great bull did not care to receive another. With a harsh bellow of rage and anguish he turned, plunged into the underwood, and disappeared.

The whole forest seemed to quake as he went.

While all this was happening, Shasta, crouched behind his tree, had watched with intense excitement the progress of the fight. Now that Gomposh had proved himself conqueror, and that the moose had disappeared, he came out from his refuge.

He wanted to thank Gomposh, to make him feel how glad he was that he had beaten the moose. But for some reason peculiar to himself, Gomposh evidently did not want to be thanked. And when Shasta went up to lay his hand on his thick black coat, he rumbled something rude in his chest and moved sulkily away. As he went he turned once to look back at the boy, and then, like the moose, disappeared among the trees.

Left alone on the spot where the great battle had been fought, and where he had come so near losing his life, Shasta looked about him carefully. The ground was torn up and tram-

WITH A HARSH BELLOW OF RAGE AND ANGUISH HE PLUNGED
INTO THE UNDERWOOD

pled, the grass and leaves blotched with dark stains. A faint smell of newly-spilt blood filled the air. And all round crowded the trees, dark, solemn, full of unnamable things.

As Shasta watched, a feeling of dread came over him. He could not have explained the feeling. All he knew was that it was a bad place where bad things could happen, and where even Gomposh had not cared to remain. Without lingering another moment, he fled away on noiseless naked feet.

And down in the cedar swamp, among the skunk cabbage and the bad black pools, old Gomposh sat in his lair and licked his wound. It did not heal for several days; but the big slavery tongue kept busily at work, and Nature, the old unfailing nurse, attended to her job. A good deal of grumbling accompanied the licking, and acted like a tongue on Gomposh's mind. So it was not long before he went about as usual, and the nuthatches perceived that Gomposh was so very much Gomposh again that the toadstools were being punished for having grown so fat!

SHASTA LEAVES HIS WOLF KIN

CHAPTER XIV

THE days and weeks went by. By the time the dark blue flower of the camass had faded, and the yellow wild parsley had begun to look tired, Shasta began to feel again the same strange restlessness creeping over him which he had felt before. And whenever he turned his face towards the southeast, the remembrance of the Indian village would sit down thickly upon him, and he would stop to think. When he remembered the raw-hide lariat and the husky dogs, he hated the camp; but when he remembered with his nose-memory, the pleasant odour of the burning cottonwood and of the dried sweet-grass came to him and made a stirring in his heart. Moreover, the Indian smell was there—the smell that does not come from cottonwood nor sweet-grass, or parfleches filled with buffalo meat, but clings about even the Indian

[205]

names and is an odour of the old, forgotten
times.

And as he went along the trails, somehow
or other everything was different. The birds
were there just the same. The blue jays were
full of jabbering talk. The crows followed
each other from tree to tree, always crying to
those ahead to go farther on, and fasten their
food-bags to another bough. And the wood-
pecker hammered hollowly at the hidden heart
of the woods. As with the birds, so with
the beasts. Nitka and Shoomoo went and
came on the hunting trails, and the wolf-
brothers howled in the night. Gomposh
slapped the dead logs for grubs, and was a silly
old bear when nobody was watching. But
when he met any one he would sit down heavily at once and look dreadfully wise. And the
weasels went on their wicked ways, killing and
killing, not because of hunger, but the blood-
lust to kill. And the red squirrels and the
grey squirrels ran along the tree-tops for
miles, without ever coming to ground; and the
fussy little chipmunks fussed.

Yet in spite of all this, Shasta felt that something had changed, and that nothing could ever be quite the same again. And although the wolves brought him just as much meat as before, so that he never went hungry, he kept longing for the taste of the buffalo tongue which the Indian woman had thrown to him out of the smoking pot. The wolves never brought him anything so good as that. It made his mouth water whenever he thought of that delicious thing.

So he wandered up and down, up and down, more and more restless, and difficult to satisfy. It was not that he was unhappy. Sometimes, even, he was wildly happy, running and leaping in the sun, or swinging on a fir branch, and talking wolf-talk to himself. At such times the sunlight and the sweet mountain air seemed to have got into his blood, and the blue sky did not seem blue enough or the moss green enough, or the Bargloosh big enough, to be equal to his joy. It was the life that was in him which could not contain itself in his body, and kept overflowing the high brim of his heart!

Yet the creatures and their ways did not

wholly satisfy him. That was the mischief of it. There were other creatures and other ways. He had seen those other creatures and he could not forget. He did not know that they were his own people, and that the drawing which he felt towards them was blood, and not cooked buffalo tongue. When his thoughts ran that way, it was the remembrance of the *smell* and the *taste* of the new life that was strongest. Even the memory of the lariat and the huskies could not overcome that. And as Meeko, the red squirrel, was always running along the green roof of the world, chickering and making mischief, and egging folks on to fight, so along the roof of Shasta's mind the new restlessness ran, and chickered, and would not let him be.

The morning came at last when he bowed his head and obeyed. He stood a long time at the mouth of the cave, looking over the familiar world of forest and mountain, and the distant shining peaks. Far away to the south he saw a speck against the blue. It moved slowly as he watched. Something told him that it was Kennebec, sitting in the wind. Kennebec had

been very quiet of late. Now that there were
no eaglets to feed, there was not so much need
to go cub and lamb snatching on the mountain
slopes. Besides which, he avoided the Bargloosh. It was there that the creature lived
who had dared to scale his rocks. Henceforth
the Bargloosh became for Kennebec a place of
danger, and he gave it a wide berth.

Now, as Shasta gazed over the wide spaces
below him, and up at the rocks above, he looked
at them wistfully, as if he were saying good-
bye. He didn't know anything about good-
bye really, because the animals never con-
sciously say farewell. They separate from
each other because their feet take them, but
it is mercifully hidden from them that sometimes they will not return. Something in him
begged him to stay: to remain where he was
and not mix himself up with the new, unexplained life that was busy among the foot-
hills, where there were lariats and husky dogs,
and where the creatures walked on their hind
legs. Here he knew the world and the ways
of all its folk. From the shadowy inside of
the cave to the glare of the sunlight on the

shimmering peaks, he was familiar with it all; it was built about his heart in a bigness that was home. But now, for some unexplained and mysterious reason he was leaving it and going to this other utterly different thing which had bound him and bitten him and had given new smells to his nose and a new taste to his tongue. And he knew perfectly well that neither Nitka nor Shoomoo, nor any of the wolf-brothers would wish him to go; just as clearly as if they all sat on their haunches in a row in front of him and implored him to remain. They were all away now, and he was alone at the den's mouth. But if they should come back before he started, he knew that he could not keep the thing a secret from their sharp understandings. They would lick him, and rub noses, and look at him out of their wild wonderful eyes, and say, "*We* know, Little Person!" and then the thing would be impossible, and he would not be able to go.

In a moment he had run swiftly down the slope and was lost among the trees.

The sun was setting when he reached the end of the canyon towards the Indian camp.

He did not go by way of the wolf-rocks this time. It was there that Looking-All-Ways had seized him, and he did not want to be caught like that again. So he had climbed down the steep sides of the gorge which the Indians call Big Wolf Canyon, and crept out among the high clumps of bunch-grass beside the stream. He could not see the village from here. It was hidden by a swell of the ground; but though he could not see it, he caught the sounds and the smells of it as they drifted down-wind. Presently he plucked up his courage and climbed to the top of the rising ground. Here the village was full in view. Soft blue trails of smoke were rising from the tops of the lodges, for the squaws were preparing the evening meal. The camp looked very peaceful, and not at all a thing to fill you with dread. Nevertheless, Shasta eyed it suspiciously, as a thing full of unexpected dangers which yelped and had sharp teeth.

Slowly he crept forward, crawling from tuft to tuft of grass, and taking advantage of every bit of rising ground, so that he might approach as close as possible without being seen. The things he was particularly on his guard against were the huskies; but as luck would have it, there was not a single dog on this side of the camp, so that he crept right up to the outer circle of lodges without any mishap. It was not till he had reached the inner circle of lodges and was crouching at the back of one of them that he was discovered.

The one who made the discovery was no less a person than Running-Laughing, the ten-year-old daughter of the chief. She was carrying a buffalo bag to fetch water from the stream, and passed so close behind the tepee that she almost trod on Shasta before she saw him. She stood still in amazement, looking down at the strange thing at her feet. Shasta gazed at her in equal astonishment, but also with fear. By reason of his position on the ground Running-Laughing looked taller to him than she really was. He marvelled at her appearance, and the things she seemed to have stuck on to her skin. It is true she only wore a soft-tanned buckskin dress, trimmed with porcupine quills and deer-bones, and had small white shells in her ears; but to Shasta's unaccustomed eyes it was a wonderful and very dreadful gear. As for him, he was just as he was and was neatly dressed in his own skin, which was a reddish-brown under the fine hair.

For some time they looked at each other without a sound or a movement. Then Running-Laughing behaved like her name, and told her father, Big Eagle, what she had found.

Big Eagle was preparing for a religious service in the lodge of the Yellow Buffalo. When he heard that the wolf-child was again in the camp, he sent for Looking-All-Ways to tell him that his captive had returned.

Looking-All-Ways went at once with Running-Laughing to where Shasta crouched beside the tepee. When he came there, he did not attempt to touch Shasta, but he carried the raw-hide lariat with him in case of need. He did something even wiser. He sent Running-Laughing to find Shoshawnee, the medicine-man, and tell him to come. So Running-Laughing fetched Shoshawnee, and when he came he began to "make medicine" with his voice.

Now, to "make medicine" with your voice is

not an easy thing to do, and is only to be done by those who know forest-lore, and prairie-lore, and the secrets of the beasts. And Shoshawnee could do this, because he was crammed full of lore, and his head was bulging with buffalo wisdom and a knowledge of the beasts. As regards the beasts, he did not, of course, know as much as Shasta did, but he knew quite enough to make him wiser than the other Indians, and directly he began to talk, Shasta *knew* that he knew!

It was a wonderful and strange "medicine" which Shoshawnee made; and if you understood the Indian tongue you would have heard many beautiful and far-away things. For in the Indian medicine-talk there are many and many words which come a long way from the North and a long way from the South, and very far indeed from the East and West. From the North they fall, as the feathers drop from the wings of wild geese, when they come honk-honking in the deep nights. From the South they are of the buffalo where they wallow by the great lake whose waters never rest. From the East they are of the coyotes, and from the West of the wolves. And many other sounds there are, too, and words which make you think of the wind along the scarped edges of rocks, and of the rumble of avalanches as they fall thunderously, and of the whisper of the junipers when the air creeps. All the great wilderness seemed to give itself in echoes along Shoshawnee's tongue.

As Shasta listened, a peculiar feeling came upon him. The sound of Shoshawnee's speaking affected him as nothing had done before. It seemed to rub him gently all over with a soothing touch. Deep within him something answered to it, and was pleased. His fear and distrust of the Indians melted away under the influence of the voice. The look of the wild animal in his eyes began to soften into something that was almost human. Shoshawnee saw the effect which the medicine was producing, and went on.

Gradually he began to move away from the tepee. As he did so, he walked backwards, keeping his eyes always fixed upon Shasta, and holding him with his gaze. Shasta looked straight into Shoshawnee's eyes. The eyes were like the voice. They drew him, whether he wanted them to or no. Slowly, step by step, he left the tepee and began to follow the medicine-man in his slow backward walk. Where he was going and why he was doing this he had no idea. Only the voice called him, and the eyes drew. He must follow those eyes and that voice wherever they chose to go.

By degrees Shoshawnee moved into the centre of the camp, Shasta following him a few feet away. Not many paces off, the lodge of the Yellow Buffalo was pitched. Inside sat Big Eagle and his braves, collected for the sacred ceremony. The ceremony had not yet begun, because they were waiting for the medicine-man to sing the opening words, without which the "medicine" of the buffaloes would not be complete.

At last Shoshawnee entered the lodge, still walking backwards. In a moment or two Shasta followed. He saw the braves sitting on the ground with Big Eagle in the centre. For the moment they were not saying or doing anything. There seemed to be a great number, for the tepee was full. Just in front of

[216]

Big Eagle there burnt a small fire. After Shoshawnee and Shasta had entered and Shoshawnee had sat down, Big Eagle took an ember from the fire with a forked stick. He then put some dried sweet-grass on it, to burn. Soon the smoke of the burning grass filled the lodge with a pleasant smell. Shasta sniffed this new smell up his nose with delight. He watched the grey threads of smoke with wonder. He thought they must be the wings of the ember which it waved in the air. Presently Big Eagle put his hands in the smoke and rubbed them over his body. Shasta looked on in astonishment. To him, hands were fore-paws. He had never seen fore-paws do so much, or do it in so odd a way.

When Big Eagle had rubbed himself all over with sweet smoke, he took another ember and with it lit a large pipe. The pipe was of polished stone, and red in colour.

Then Shasta saw what to him was the most surprising thing of all. When Big Eagle had put the red thing to his mouth, a wing came out and waved itself in the air! The pipe went from mouth to mouth, as the braves passed it round the lodge, and from every mouth, as it went, grey wings sprouted, and went wandering through the air.

After the smoking was over, the ceremony began. Shasta heard Shoshawnee make many strange noises, and let his voice run up and down as if he wanted to howl. It made Shasta want to howl also, but he remembered that he was not among the wolves now, and so he kept the feeling down.

When Shoshawnee had finished, the other braves went on. They seemed to want to howl badly too! Shasta could not understand how they could make so many odd noises in their throats, and yet never throw their heads back for the long sobbing note. On each side of Big Eagle were the squaws Lillooeet and Sarvis, his two wives. They had rattles in their hands, and they beat them on a buffalo hide stretched upon the floor. The beating was in time to the chanting, and Shasta watched in wonderment the rise and fall of the rattles, which, every time they touched the hide, gave out a sharp noise.

Presently, at a signal from Big Eagle, the

rattling ceased. Shoshawnee rose. He advanced three paces towards Shasta. Then he stretched out his hand and laid it on his head. When Shasta felt the hand of Shoshawnee upon his head the tingling feeling ran in his blood and made his flesh creep. Then Shoshawnee spoke. What he said Shasta could not understand, yet it seemed to him that, as he had once been admitted to the wolf-pack as of its blood, now he was being received into the Indian pack as one of themselves. And he was right in his guess, for this is what Shoshawnee said:

"This is Shasta, the wolf-child. I have tamed him, because I understand the wolf-medicine. But he *is* the wolf-medicine! Because of that, he is stronger than I."

There was a pause here, while the whole company gathered together in the tepee gazed at Shasta with awe. Presently Shoshawnee went on:

"Many moons ago, the Assiniboines, as you know, attacked us when we were moving to the Sakuska river to pitch our summer camp. A squaw was killed, and her papoose carried off.

The brave who did this was not an Assiniboine. He was Red Fox, who stole the Eagle medicine, and is a traitor to our tribe. Red Fox went to the Assiniboines with lies upon his tongue. But the papoose which Red Fox carried off was the grandson of Fighting Bull, our old chief, who died soon afterwards. And his name was Shasta, which is one of our oldest names. Nothing was afterwards seen of the papoose in the lodges of the Assiniboines. Why? I will tell you. Because its father had been his deadly enemy, Red Fox gave it to the wolves!"

Shoshawnee suddenly ceased speaking; but his eyes glowed, and the echo of his voice seemed to run in the ears of the braves, as if his thought, which was fierce and strong, made itself a voice out of the silence.

HOW SHASTA FOUGHT MUSHA-WUNK

CHAPTER XV

HOW SHASTA FOUGHT MUSHA-WUNK

SO that was how it came to pass that Shasta was received by the Indians into their tribe, and was called by his own name, which he had never known. The moons went by, and by degrees he left off his wolf-ways and took on Indian ways instead. He learnt to walk upright, to eat cooked food and to talk the Indian tongue. To learn the last took him a long time. At first he could only make wolf noises, and would growl when he was angry, bark when he was excited, and howl when it was necessary to say things to the moon. But he had Shoshawnee for teacher, and Shoshawnee's patience had no end. At first he was shy of the Indian boys, because they teased him when they had opportunity, and their elders' backs were turned; but by degrees his shyness wore away, and he began to take part in their racing and riding.

Soon he could ride and run races with the best of them. Also, when it came to wrestling, they soon found that he was more than their match; for his life among the wolves had given an extraordinary strength to his muscles and suppleness to his body.

It was in a fight with Musha-Wunk that this quality of Shasta's body first made itself known. Musha-Wunk was a bully, and one of the leaders of those who enjoyed teasing Shasta whenever they had a chance. So one day Musha-Wunk and his companions came upon Shasta when he was sitting by himself amongst the bunch-grass of the creek.

At first, when Musha-Wunk began to tease and probe him with a stick, Shasta pretended not to mind, and got up and walked away.

Even when Musha-Wunk followed and stabbed him again, he took it all in good part, and caught hold of the stick with a laugh. But Musha-Wunk snatched the stick away with a vicious pull and struck Shasta with it across the face.

What followed came so quickly that those who watched held their breath in astonishment.

[224]

How Shasta Fought Musha-Wunk

The leap of a wolf is so swift that it must be seen to be believed. When Shasta leaped on the bully, the other boys saw something that seemed to hurl itself through the air, strike savagely, and bound away. Musha-Wunk, taken utterly by surprise, went down under the blow. He was on his feet in an instant, but almost before he was up, Shasta had hurled himself on him again. This time Musha-Wunk seized him before he could leap away, and both boys rolled over together. Musha-Wunk was the heavier of the two. He had bigger bones and a more powerful body. If he could have held Shasta down, he would certainly have had the best of it. But to hold Shasta down was like sitting on a small volcano. There was a violent eruption of arms and legs, and Musha-Wunk was lifted into the air! While he was still struggling to his feet, Shasta was on him again.

It was the wolf in Shasta which urged him to these lightning attacks and counter-attacks which made the eyes blink. Once the wild-beast spirit in him was fully roused, nothing could stand against it. The wolf-blood raced in his veins; the wolf-light flashed in his eyes. There broke out of his throat fierce sounds which certainly were not human. As he fought, he seemed to himself to be a wolf again, with the uncontrollable wolf-fury raging in his heart. Yet it was not merely wild rage that was in him. At the back of his mind, he knew that he was fighting for his freedom, for his self-respect. Once he allowed himself to be beaten by Musha-Wunk, he knew that the other boys would have no mercy upon him.

The time for gentleness and forbearance was gone by. The fight was none of his making. Musha-Wunk had forced it upon him, because he was a bully, and because he had judged Shasta to be a coward. The other boys stood round in a silent ring, watching the fight with glittering eyes. Their very silence showed how deeply they were moved; though, Indian-like, they gave no vent to their feeling by any outward sign. They were like a circle of animals, watching, with a fierce animal joy, a combat waged to the death. And presently a terror, as of death itself, came to Musha-Wunk, the bully, as he fought. He had thought that

to conquer Shasta would be a very easy thing.
He wanted to give him a good thrashing, see
the blood flow, and leave the wolf-boy half
dead at the finish. But now he knew, when
too late, that he had roused something which
it was not in his power to subdue. By his own
folly and cruelty, he had drawn upon himself
a vengeance which was not of men, but of the
wolves. He ceased to take the offensive. All
he wanted now was to defend himself as best
he could against Shasta's lightning attacks.
It was when he tried to hold Shasta that the
marvellous elasticity of the wolf-boy's body
showed itself. No matter how Musha-Wunk
bent it this way and that, straining every muscle till the veins stood out on his throat, Shasta's firm flesh and wonderful sinews resisted
every effort to break him into submission. He
twirled himself into the most astonishing po-
sitions, upsetting Musha-Wunk every time the
bully seemed for a moment to have gained the
upper hand.

The fight finished as suddenly as it had begun. Musha-Wunk had received so severe a
punishing that at last he could bear it no

longer. It was not his body alone that suffered. In his mind the terror was growing. It was a horrible feeling that what he fought was a boy outwardly only, and was in reality more than half a wolf! The sudden leap, the break away, the deadly leap again—this was how the wolves fought. It was not to be met in any familiar human way. Taking advantage of a moment when Shasta seemed to pause, Musha-Wunk turned and fled towards the camp.

The other Indian boys looked on in astonishment at this ending to the fight. They would hardly believe their eyes that the big and masterful Musha-Wunk should be defeated so utterly by the little wolf-boy that at last he should flee in terror. They gazed at Shasta, the victor, in awe, keeping a respectful distance for fear lest the wolf in him might turn suddenly upon them. It did not need Shasta's quick eyes to perceive this fear upon them; his mind caught it as it oozed, in spite of themselves, into the air. Swift, as always, to act when his mind had once clearly seen a thing, he made a quick step forward, crouching as if to spring. To the alarmed Indian boys it seemed as if his whole body quivered with rage. In its crouching position it seemed to take on itself mysteriously the actual outlines of a wolf. Certainly the eyes between the long and shaggy locks of hair shot out a light that was not human, but of that deep brute world, old and savage, in the thick lair of the trees.

It was enough. Without waiting an instant longer, the whole band broke asunder and took to their heels in flight.

Shasta watched their departure with a joyful triumph. Now at last he had proved that the wolf-spirit in him was not to be broken, and that those who provoked or insulted it did so at their own peril. It was the upright, free spirit of the wild. And as such it was a good spirit, and belonged to the early freshness of the world. In Shasta, it would not attack or injure things as long as they left him alone. But once his freedom or peace were threatened, then he would resist with all the strength in his power.

When the last flying form had disappeared

behind the rising ground, Shasta turned towards the trees. The excitement that was in him danced and bubbled in his blood. He was tired and sore in his body, but his heart was high—high as the tops of the spruces and the pines. He felt that he must go and tell his heart to the trees.

He went far into the forest, and then sat down. The trees were all about him—close on every side. It was as if they were crowding up to him to hear what he had to say. The big silence of them did not make him lonely or afraid. They were solemn and yet companionable, and full of wise "medicine"—which he understood, but could not put into speech.

The Indian camp was very far away now. Musha-Wunk and the others were little things that did not matter. It was the trees that mattered now—the trees and the wolves.

Only his fine ear could have detected that soft footfall coming down the trail! And when he turned his eyes, it did not surprise him that he looked straight into those of a big grey wolf.

What Shasta said to the wolf and what the

wolf said to Shasta cannot be set down in words. Though it was neither Nitka nor Shoomoo, it was a wolf-brother of three seasons back, and the two recognized each other in some mysterious way. And so Shasta was able to learn all he wanted to know about the den upon the Bargloosh, and how his foster-parents fared. It was over nine months now since he had seen them, but, according to the wolf-brother, nothing was amiss. Upon the Bargloosh everything went much as it had gone in the old days when Shasta was a little naked man-cub, and had no notion of wearing clothes. The wolf-brother did not approve of the clothing Shasta wore, though it was only a little tanned buckskin tunic falling to the knee. For that was one of Shasta's peculiarities, that though he suffered the upper part of his body to be clad, he would not allow them to interfere with the freedom of his legs. Moccasins he would only wear in winter, when the frost bit hard, or in the summer when he had a fit upon him to decorate his feet. Running-Laughing had made him the summer moccasins, and had embroidered them most cunningly with elk-teeth and porcupine quills. Shasta walked stiffly, with a sense of grandeur, when he wore the summer moccasins, looking down at his feet as if they belonged to some great medicine-man or important chief.

The wolf-brother sniffed at the tunic disapprovingly. The Indian smell of it upset him, and made his hackles rise. So Shasta, to please him, took it off, and let him see that it was only a loose skin that did not matter, and could easily be thrown away. After that things went more smoothly, and they talked companionably together in the shadow of the trees. And when the evening light began to be golden about the tops of the spruces, and the forest to stir, and shake off the drowsy weight of the afternoon, the wolf-brother departed as suddenly and softly as he had come, and Shasta, having watched him go regretfully, turned homewards to the camp.

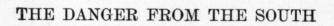

THE DANGER FROM THE SOUTH

CHAPTER XVI

THE DANGER FROM THE SOUTH

IT was the old medicine-man, Shoshawnee, and he was making medicine to himself on the high lookout butte that commanded the prairies to the south. The sunset was beginning to be crimson in the west. It struck full in Shoshawnee's face, turning it blood-red. But Shoshawnee had no thought for the colour of his face. He had another thought inside him—a thought of such tremendous importance that there was no room for anything besides. And this was that a danger lay there ambushed in the south. No one else but Shoshawnee knew of the danger; but that was because he had a medicine which never told him lies, and which whispered things to him before they had arrived. And already it had whispered to him that danger was near, and he had heard the huskies give the ghost-bark when they saw the wind go by.

When he had finished the medicine-song he sat silent, gazing on the prairies. They looked very peaceful, lying abroad there under the sinking sun. Shoshawnee's eyes, travelling over the immense levels, saw nothing that served to increase the unquiet of his mind. Far to the south there stretched, from the Saska River westwards, a dusky band that was like a shadow cast by the sunset. Shoshawnee knew that it was a herd of buffalo—one of those vast herds which in those old Indian days roamed over the wilderness for a thousand miles; coming always from the lake of mystery in the south; going no man knew whither; which no man had ever counted, or would count till the Palefaces came from the East, and the Red man's day was done. Shoshawnee watched the buffaloes keenly. So long as they continued their tranquil feeding, he knew that, whatever danger was afoot, it had not yet approached the outskirts of the herd. For the buffalo are very wary and are always ready to stampede. Yet, although his eyes were fixed intently out there so many miles away, his ears were alert for anything that might happen close about. So, although he did not turn his head, he heard the faint whisper of the dried bent-grass as Shasta in his summer moccasins came lightly up the hill.

When he reached Shoshawnee, Shasta did not speak. It is the Palefaces who rush at each other with their tongues. The Red man is never in a hurry with his speech. Why should you hasten your words when the prairies are so broad beside you, and there are no clocks to tick off for you the timeless drift of the summer air? It is only in the cities that men have learnt to waste the hours by counting them; and on the high buttes facing the sunset there is no time.

So the sun had dipped below the prairie before at last Shoshawnee spoke.

"The buffalo go west," he said slowly, as if the thing was of the utmost importance.

Shasta did not put a question actually into words, but he looked it. Shoshawnee understood.

"There is much pasture to the west. The buffalo eat the prairie to the setting sun."

[237]

"Do they eat the edge of the sunset also?" Shasta asked.

Shoshawnee shook his head.

"The edge of the sunset is the end of the world," he said. "At the end of all things there is no more grass."

Shasta was silent at that. It was so unbelievable. The thought stunned him. No more grass!

"But *beyond* the sunset," Shoshawnee went on, "when you come to the Happy Hunting-grounds, the grass is always green. And there the blue flower of the camass never fades, and the sarvis berries never decay."

"The Happy Hunting-grounds!" Shasta murmured in his low, husky voice. "Where?"

Shoshawnee lifted his hand.

"Up there, presently," he said, "you will see the Wolf-trail. It is along the Wolf-trail that you travel to reach them. The Wolf-trail is worn across the heavens by the moccasins of the dead."

"Is the hunting better there than it is here?" Shasta asked. "Is there more game?"

"It is not *better* hunting," Shoshawnee said,

[238]

correcting him. "It is happier. The dead
are full of happiness as they follow along the
trail."

After that there was a long silence, as Shasta
kept looking at the sky to watch for the beginning of the Wolf-trail, when the stars
should appear. But before that happened
Shoshawnee spoke again. This time he spoke
quickly, using many words. He spoke so rapidly, and the words followed each other so fast,
that at first Shasta could not understand. All
he gathered was that danger was in the air,
some great danger which as yet you could not
see, but which was approaching, always drawing steadily nearer out there on the prairies,
and which might arrive before you knew.
Then, as Shoshawnee went on, the danger took
a shape. It was the shape of Indians on the
warpath—Assiniboines that came with deadly
cunning and purpose, travelling like wolves
along the prairie hollows.

Shasta sent his eyes far across the darken-
ing plains, where all things were becoming
shadowy and remote, and where even the great
herd of buffalo beyond the Saska was no longer

visible. How far away the Assiniboines might be he could not guess. Nor could Shoshawnee tell him, when he asked. All Shoshawnee knew was that they were coming, and that when he had finished his medicine-making he would go and warn the tribe. Of one thing only was he certain, and that was, that however near they might be they would not attack at night. The Assiniboines were fierce and cruel but they dreaded the darkness, because they declared that the ghosts of their enemies and many evil spirits were abroad. Their favourite hour of attack was just at daybreak when the first glimmer of dawn was mingling with the mist.

When the last light of sunset had faded from the sky, and the prairies were wholly dark, Shasta and Shoshawnee returned to the camp.

Shasta lay awake long that night, listening and wondering. The words of the old medicine-man kept walking in his head. Sometimes it was of the buffaloes he thought, with their pasture that lay out into the sunset and was a-shimmer with the long lights of the west; and sometimes of that mysterious danger that crept nearer and nearer, and gave no sign of its approach. And then the butterfly, the sleep-bringer, flitted across his eyelids and he slept.

It was the western lark-sparrow that woke him in the morning, singing loud and clear upon the lodge-pole over his head. And when he saw the sunlight clear through the painted wall of the tepee, and heard the cheerful morning stir of the camp, it seemed impossible that danger should be afoot in that tremendous peace. Yet, as the day wore on and evening drew near, he felt the same foreboding at his heart as when Shoshawnee had spoken to him of danger when they sat on the lookout bluff.

As for Shoshawnee, he sat there all day, without food or drink, gazing steadily across the prairies and chanting the old medicine chants of the tribe. When evening fell Shoshawnee returned. He had already warned the tribe of what he feared, and Big Eagle had given orders that all was to be in readiness in case of an attack. Scouts had been sent out, but had returned at sundown, saying that no signs of hostile Indians had been seen.

Shasta of the Wolves

When Shasta went to bed that night the buffalo robe held no sleep for him; and wherever the butterfly flitted, it did not enter his tepee. All night long he lay awake, restless and uneasy. Often and often he left his couch and looked out. The camp was very still and the stars in their high places glittered bright in a cloudless sky. Now and then the small grey owl hooted dismally from the alder thickets beside the creek, or a coyote would bark fitfully somewhere far off in the night. Shasta had not yet grown used to the prairie. It was so vast, so unenclosed! The forest with its crowding trees, and the immense gloom of a hundred miles of shade, was the thing that made him feel at home. But now the camp of his people was pitched far out on the prairie, and the forest only existed in his dreams. As for Nitka and Shoomoo and the wolf-brothers, they seemed even farther off, and to move in some old life lost among the trees. Three times already since his first coming to the camp, it had been moved. The ends of the new lodge-poles, cut in spring among the foot-hills and dragged by the ponies for enormous distances, now showed signs of wear. The camp at present lay in a wide hollow surrounded by swelling ridges, and hidden from sight until you were close upon it. The lookout bluff upon which Shoshawnee had kept his watch lay a good half-mile to the south, and commanded an immense sweep of prairie on every hand.

The last time Shasta had crept out of the tepee he had looked towards the bluff. It humped itself, a black mass against the stars, like a huge bull-buffalo couched in sleep. When he crept noiselessly back, it seemed to follow him, and when at last sleep overtook him, it was humped among his dreams.

Suddenly he was wide awake, his heart throbbing. Something—he did not know what —had called to him, and roused him from his rest. The tepee was still dark, but a faint glimmer—so faint as to be scarcely seen— showed that daybreak was at hand. Shasta sat up, his eyes straining in the dimness, and his ears listening as only wild animals listen when they are startled.

For a little while he heard nothing but the stillness, which itself was so deep that it seemed as if it were a sort of sound. Then, clear and strikingly distinct, he heard repeated the sound which had broken his sleep.

It was a wolf-howl, long-drawn and wailing, and it was answered directly afterwards by another, and yet another. The cries were some distance off—how far Shasta could not tell. The third came from some spot on the prairie beyond the lookout bluff.

Every pulse in Shasta's body beat in answer to the cries. A wild excitement swept through him. His mind seemed, for the moment, to throw off its Indian teaching and swing back into the wild. Yet, wolf-like though the cries were—so alike that only the wolves themselves would have detected the difference—Shasta's perfect sense of hearing told him that these wailing notes came from no wolf-throats, but from those of Indians who imitated with marvellous closeness the familiar cry. Shoshawnee was right. The danger was at hand. It was within speaking distance: it sang a death-note in the dawn.

Shasta lost no time. He ran swiftly to Big Eagle's tepee. Without waiting for any ceremony, he snatched aside the flap and stepped inside. Rousing the chief he told him what he had heard. Immediately Big Eagle sprang from his buffalo robes, and, seizing his arms, rushed out into the centre of the camp, uttering the gathering cry. Instantly the whole camp was aroused. The braves came running out of the tepees, their bows in their hands and their long quivers slung over their backs. In less than five minutes the sleeping village was turned into an armed camp, with every man it contained prepared for the fight. In the midst of the excitement Shasta disappeared. When Big Eagle commanded the presence of the "medicine" wolf-boy, no one could say what had become of him. Some were inclined to think that he had played a trick upon them, and that there was no danger at all. But Shoshawnee, the old medicine-man, waved his arms excitedly, and declared over and over again that Shasta had been warned by the spirits, and that the Assiniboines were now close at hand.

SHASTA GOES SCOUTING

CHAPTER XVII

SHASTA GOES SCOUTING

WHEN Shasta had given the warning and knew that the tribe was fully roused, he crept out of camp. He went so secretly that no one saw him go. Why he went he could hardly have told himself in the shape of a thought. If the cries had not been wolf-cries, it is probable he would not have gone. He was certain that they were not the genuine wolf-calls, yet they came so very close to them that an uneasy feeling inside him made him want to find out what sort of throat could make so exact an imitation.

The direction of his going was towards the lookout butte, from beyond which the last cry had come. If danger was gathering in the prairie hollows it would be from the summit of the butte that you could tell the nature of it, and whether it was widespread or closely

drawn. As he approached the butte, his eyes
and ears were open at their widest. Things
were indistinct and shadowy in the faint glimmer of the dawn. Yet shadowy though they
were, Shasta's piercing eyes stabbed them
through and through. Every bush, every
clump of grass, every rise or fall of the ground
—nothing escaped this piercing gaze. He saw
the buck-rabbit leap into the thicket. He saw
the coyote drift, like a trail of grey smoke,
over the ridge. And while his eyes and ears
were busy, he did not forget his nose. With
the true wolf-instinct he travelled up-wind.
Whatever scents were abroad in the keen air,
he would catch them surely, and sift them in
his cunning nose. In the early freshness of
the dawn, the smell of the ground was sweet
with dew. There was not so much a breeze as
a soft moving of the air. Along it the whole
vast body of the prairie seemed to breathe to
the tip of Shasta's nose. By this time the
broad sweet prairie smell was familiar to him.
By contrast with it the old smells of the forest
seemed to be sharp and thin, like arrow-heads
piercing the brain. But, as Shasta knew, this

broader prairie smell was made up of a countless multitude of tiny odours that mixed themselves so confusedly that only the stronger ones
could be disentangled from the rest.

For some time he did not get any smell which
told him of danger, and he had reached the foot
of the butte before he met anything suspicious.
Suddenly he stopped.   As far as you could see
or hear, except that the light was a little
stronger, everything was exactly as it had been.
And yet, to Shasta's quick sense, something
had happened, and he knew that he was
warned.   It was not that he saw or heard anything first.   It was his nose which had caught
something that was not a prairie smell.   It
was not of a thing that was there now.   The
thing had gone by, but the scent of its passing
clung still to the grass-blades, and Shasta
seemed to *see* the Indian body which had left
that faint message of itself in smell.   Then he
found the trail—the dim thing that only wild
eyes would see as it lay in the morning twilight.

At first he wondered what to do, whether to
follow the track or to go up the butte.   He
knew that whatever he did must be done at

once, or he might be too late. He went swiftly
up the butte.

When he reached the top he lay at full
length, gazing intently over the prairies. In
the pale light of the creeping dawn, they looked
wider than ever. They seemed to stretch
away and away endlessly, as if the world did
not cease at the horizon, but stooped down
under the sky. Shasta's eyes swept that huge
greyness with a lightning glance. The hollows
lay roughly from northeast to southwest. It
was only here and there that it was possible to
see their bottoms or what might be concealed
along the borders of the streams.

For some minutes Shasta saw nothing suspicious. Then, about two hundred yards to
the west, he saw a creeping shape move across
the top of a ridge and disappear. It was followed by another and then another. They slid
very quickly over the open summit of the
ridge. At the very first glance he knew they
were not wolves.

He watched a great number pass over in that
peculiar sliding way. When there was a
pause, and no more seemed to be coming,

Shasta turned to leave the butte. What he saw as he did so made his heart leap.

There, not twenty yards away from the foot of the butte, stood an Indian, with his bow in his hand, ready to shoot.

At once Shasta realized that it was a stranger, one of the hostile tribe about to attack the camp. While his mind worked swiftly, deciding what to do, his body never moved a muscle. There he was, crouched upon the butte, as motionless as if he had been suddenly turned to stone.

If he attempted to escape the Indian by running east or west, he knew by the way the brave held his bow that a terrible winged shaft would come singing through the air. The Indians had evidently seen him on the butte, and one of them had been told off to watch that he did not return to camp to carry a warning before the attack was made. By creeping to the top of the butte in order to reconnoitre the outer prairies, Shasta saw that he had exposed himself to a hidden danger behind. He saw himself cut off from the camp, utterly alone. He had already given warning, it is true. But his people might not know that the enemy were so close upon them, nor how many were gathering for the attack. And whatever happened, he would be utterly powerless to help them in the fight with their relentless foes. A feeling of desperation, of anger, swept over him. It was like the anger which had wrapped its flames about him when he had turned on Musha-Wunk, the bully.

Suddenly, in a flash, he turned and darted over the brow of the hill. Instantly the Indian shot, but Shasta had been too quick for him, and the arrow buried itself in the hillside. Shasta was hidden now by the hill, and the Indian could not tell which way he had gone. The boy went down the hill at a tremendous pace in a series of flying bounds. When he reached the bottom he turned sharp to the left. There was broken ground here, and a number of thickets. Threading his way cautiously through these, Shasta worked eastwards, meaning to approach the camp from the far northeastern side. He had not gone very far when he heard a series of war-whoops, followed by savage yells, and he knew that the battle had begun. He regretted now that he had not brought his bow and arrows with him. His only weapon was the flint tomahawk in his belt.

There was much more light now. He could see everything clearly. But the camp was not in sight, because it was hidden in its hollow to the west. The sounds of the fight came to him plainly in the clear morning air.

There was a knoll in front of him. He ran towards it, stooping low as in his wolf days. He had only just reached it, and had thrown himself flat on his stomach, when all at once he heard the running of many feet. The sound was coming in his direction. He lay where he was, absolutely still. All at once he was surrounded by Indians. Something struck him sharply at the back of his head, and he remembered nothing more.

When he came to himself, he found himself lying across the back of an Indian pony, with a horrible aching in his head. The pony was at the gallop. He felt that he was held in his place by the rider. He could not see the rider. He saw nothing but a blur of grass that seemed

as if it billowed under him in flowing waves.
The blood in his head made a singing like
grasshoppers. There was a tightness there as
if it were going to burst. He tried to think,
but thoughts would not come. He could not
tell why he was on the pony's back. Only the
sharp smell of its sweating flanks entered his
brain as one smells things in a dream. Then
the seas of grass billowed away into nothing-
ness, and it was a blackness where lightnings
flashed.

That was all he remembered of that long
ride over the prairies, as he was carried by the
Assiniboines back to their hunting grounds in
the far northwest. It was not till many
moons afterwards that he learnt that, owing
to his warning, their attack had only partially
succeeded, and that his tribe had beaten them
off after a fierce encounter in which both sides
had lost heavily.

When the Assiniboines reached their camp,
Shasta was thrown into a tepee and left to
come to himself as best he might. It was not
long before he was forced to realize what had
happened, and knew that he was a prisoner in

the hands of the enemies of his tribe. What he did not know was that they had carried him off to kill him at their great sun-dance as a religious offering. Quite unknown to himself, his fame as a medicine-man had travelled far and wide over the prairies, and had even reached the mountains in the west. This was the wolf-medicine which had made his tribe so powerful since his coming to them. Once he could be killed, the medicine power would be destroyed also, but, as their own medicine-men assured them, it could be destroyed only by fire.

The weeks went by. He was allowed out of the tepee by day, but bound with thongs every night, so that he could not move. He was given much food in order to make him fat and pleasant for the ceremony.

As the time of the great dance grew near, the Indians redoubled their watch upon him. He was not even allowed to come out of the tepee during the day. The heat and the lack of exercise made him suffer in body and in mind. All he knew of the outside world came to him through the hides of the tepee. He would lie awake in the night, listening to the sounds that stirred abroad, and longing unspeakably to be out in the cool air under the star-glimmer and the sky. And then the moon would rise and the interior of the tepee would appear in a silver gloom.

It was at the moon-rising that Shasta's restlessness increased till it was like a flame that licked along his bones. His brain was on fire. All the pulses of his body beat in the burning of the flames. Then he would crouch, staring with bloodshot eyes that seemed as if they burnt holes in the tepee and pierced into the night. Now and then he would moan a little, or make low wolf-noises in his dry throat, but for the most part he was silent, suffering dumbly, as animals suffer, feeling the old free wolf-life tugging at his heart. Then there would come a moment when it was impossible to bear the torture in silence, and he would throw back his head and vent his misery in howl after howl.

It was small wonder if the Indians beat him for that. Those dismal notes, ringing out in the deep silence of the night, were enough to make the toughest "brave" uneasy in his heart. So each night that Shasta howled, he was beaten; and still the feeling was too strong to be overcome, and he was beaten again. Then, when it was over, and he lay panting and bruised, he would fall upon his thongs in a blind rage, striving to tear them with his teeth. But his teeth were not the fangs of Nitka, and the raw-hide thongs resisted his utmost efforts. So when dawn broke he would lie exhausted, and fall into an aching sort of slumber till they came to unbind him for the day.

Once or twice during these nightly howlings he fancied he heard an answering cry far off among the hills; and once there had been a scratching outside the tepee, and he was certain that a wolf was there. But before he could come to conversation with it an Indian had arrived to beat him, and it had slipped away.

At last the night came before the great dance that was to take place next morning at the rising of the sun. It was in the beginning of the dance that a great fire would be lighted, and that Shasta would be burned, bound fast to a

stake driven into the ground. No one told him
that this was his last night, and that it was on
the morrow that he would be killed. Yet for
all that, some instinct warned him that some
terrible thing was afoot, and that the end was
close at hand.

It was in vain that he had waited all these
weeks for his tribe to follow and rescue him.
Either they had been too severely punished by
the Assiniboines to dare to follow till they had
increased their strength, or else they had de-
layed too long and now had lost the trail. So
long he had looked for that rescue from the
southeast; and the sun had risen and set and
the moon had waxed and waned, and waxed
again, and still there had sounded through the
foot-hills no thunder of ponies' hoofs, nor
ringing war-cry as the avenging braves swept
on.

The night was very still. Moon-rise was at
hand. For two nights in succession something
had stolen to the outside of Shasta's tepee. It
had stayed only a short time, sniffing and
scratching, and then had melted into the shadowy masses of the hills. Shasta had spoken

[260]

to it. He had said very little, but then, being wolf-taught, he knew just what to say. And so the mysterious visitor had departed wiser than it came. No one saw this creature, either when it entered the camp or departed. Even the husky dogs did not detect it in their sleep. On softly-cushioned feet it glided noiselessly straight to the spot it sought; and when it had paid its visit, it seemed to float along the ground mountainwards like a trail of black mist.

And now, in a terrible suspense, Shasta was waiting, wondering if the thing would come on this, the last night, and whether its coming would bring a message of hope.

Suddenly his eyes shone and a thrill passed through him. Outside, close against the bottom of the tepee, he heard a sniff. It was the sound a wolf makes when it takes the air deeply into its lungs and then sends it out quickly. Shasta began to talk wolf-talk close to the edge of the tepee. The creature outside answered. Then, in a few moments, it melted into the night. When it was gone, Shasta felt more utterly alone than before. He was restless,

[261]

excited, nervous to a high degree. It was little
wonder if he gave voice to the pent-up wretch-
edness within him in howl after piercing howl.
They let him howl that night without beating
him, because they thought it was the last time
the "medicine"-boy would lift his wolf-voice
to the moon, and it was his death-song that he
sang.

Shasta did not howl for long at a time. He
contented himself by howling at intervals, that
were longer or shorter, as his feelings mastered
him. But presently his reason for howling
changed.

Down the long throats of the canyons between the hills there came, now in solo, now in
concert, a series of calls that set Shasta's blood
ablaze. He answered the calls time after time.
He knew every variation of them, from the
deep-throated note that was almost a bellow, to
the thin sharp call of the half-grown cub
yearning for a kill. And as Shasta sent out
his desperate messages in reply, he used every
note of the wolf-language that he knew. Up
and down the hills, wailing along the ridges,

sobbing in the hollows, went the wild cries for help, and the answering cries that help was at hand.

At daybreak the howling ceased. Over all the wilderness stole the grey silence—the silence of the dawn. Shasta, lying bound in his tepee, watched the cold light as it slowly grew. All at once, directly above his head, a clear song trilled forth. It was a lark-sparrow perched upon the top of a lodge-pole, and welcoming the day. Often and often he had listened to that song before and loved it for its gladsome sound. But then he had been safe among his own people, and free to go in and out as he chose. Now the song brought home to him afresh the sense of his loneliness and utter helplessness, bound by the cruel thongs.

The song ceased as suddenly as it had begun, and almost immediately afterwards the tepee was entered by two Indians. Without unbinding Shasta, they lifted him up and carried him outside. There he found an old white warhorse attached to a travois, or Indian carriage. Shasta had seen a travois before, but had never ridden in one. It was a sort of seat, or basket,

[263]

fastened to poles, the thin ends of which crossed in front of the horse, while the thick ends trailed along the ground. The Indians placed him on the travois and then stood beside him, waiting for the signal to start. On all sides Shasta saw that the camp was in movement. All the braves were in their war paint, and wore their big war bonnets stiff with feathers. It was plain to be seen that it was a very great occasion, and that no pains would be spared to make it a success.

THE WOLVES AVENGE

CHAPTER XVIII

THE WOLVES AVENGE

PRESENTLY, at a given sign, the procession started. It was led by an old medicine-man, who moved slowly forward, singing a medicine-chant as he walked. He was extremely old and shrivelled and was smothered in paint and feathers. And he had a husky voice that cut the air like a saw. Behind him rode the chief on horseback, a splendid figure of a man, upright as a dart, and magnificently dressed. Immediately after him came Shasta on the travois. The braves followed in a long line.

Shasta's heart was heavy with fear. No one told him what was going to be done with him, yet a terrible foreboding made him shiver now and then. And yet the birds twittered, and the air was fragrant with the scent of the dew-drenched grass, and the sky blue between the trails of mist. All the world seemed full of life, and free, except himself only, bound and aching on the travois.

When the procession reached the top of a high ridge, the travois was stopped. The Indians lifted Shasta out and bound him to a stake driven into the ground. Around the stake they piled fagots of wood. When this was finished, the medicine-man sprinkled dried sweet grass over the pile so that when the flames rose up there might be a pleasant smell. During the preparations the braves arranged themselves in a large circle about the stake. As soon as the arrangements were completed, they waited for the medicine-man to light the fire, and sing the words which would be the signal for the opening of the dance. There was a pause. For a few moments nothing happened. It was one of those strange pieces of silence which drop sometimes even into the centre of civilized life, and people become uneasy—they could not tell you why. Only the mist went on, trailing over the ridge, swaying weirdly as the air pushed. It was still cold with the freshness left by the dawn. And although the sun had already risen, his beams were not strong enough as yet to dispel the dense masses of mist that kept rising from all the lower grounds. Near or distant, so far as Shasta's keen ears could detect, nothing stirred. The fat blue grouse which had been feeding on the blueberries had fled at the Indians' approach. The old coyote who had made her den on the south side of the hill was out hunting with her young ones and had not yet returned. For any sight or sound that declared itself, the lonely ridge at the edge of the prairies was a dead lump of burnt-up summer grass where not a living creature stirred. In that tremendous pause when all the world seemed to be waiting, Shasta threw back his head and gave the long gathering-cry of the wolves.

That call for help went ringing out far from the summit of the ridge. The hollow places sucked it in, and gave back sobbing echoes of its desperate need. One long cry that was not an echo, came from the hills in answer. That was all. Then the silence of the Wild closed down, and you could hear your heart beat in

tant braves there passed a thrill that went through them like swift flame. For a second or two Shasta felt as if his heart had stopped.

At that instant, a short, deep-throated bellow came up from the mist below. It was the signal for the attack. And there was no other warning. Yet there they all were—Nitka, Shoomoo, the foster-brothers who remembered Shasta, and the other brothers who did not, and many others besides, belonging to widely-sundered packs, hundreds and hundreds of them, all united under the leadership of the giant Shoomoo for the one great purpose of rescuing Shasta from the hands of his cruel foes.

Up the sides of the ridge they bounded— those long, grey bodies that seemed buoyant like the mist.

When they reached the summit, there was not an instant's pause. In one ringing wolf-voice, the whole of the united packs gave tongue.

Already the medicine-man had taken the live coal on the stick and was just about to set it to the dried grass round the stake when he was hurled to the earth by the leaping form of a tremendous wolf—none other than Shoomoo himself!

As he fell, an Indian darted forward, intending to bury his tomahawk in the wolf. But before he could do so, Shoomoo had leaped away from the prostrate figure, and in an instant had thrown himself on his assailant. There was a gleam as the raised tomahawk caught the light. Yet though it descended it inflicted no fatal wound, and the Indian was borne helplessly to the ground, from which he never rose again.

The Indians fought desperately, but they were hopelessly outnumbered from the first. There were wolves everywhere. If one was killed or disabled, half-a-dozen more instantly filled his place. They came from all quarters, surging up from the lower ground in waves that seemed as if they would never end. On every hand the fight raged furiously. On all sides it was the same mass of dark, leaping bodies, gleaming eyes, and white fangs that tore and slashed. And everywhere it was Shoomoo, Nitka, and the wolf-brothers that did the deadliest work. Shoomoo, himself, seemed to be everywhere at once. Over and over again, Shasta, shivering, and frenzied with excitement as he watched the progress of the fight, saw the giant form of the great father wolf hurl itself through the air, and strike some struggling Indian to the ground.

Would the wolves win? Would the wolves win?—That was the agonizing thought that made Shasta shake from head to foot. If they did, he was saved. If not—then all was lost. He would be doomed to die the terrible death by fire. He wrenched and strained in a vain attempt to loose his bonds. His utmost efforts were of no avail. Whatever was the result of the contest, he knew that he must remain helpless to the end.

Once or twice a wild despair seized him. There came a pause in the fight, as if the wolves wavered. Suppose, after all, the Indians were able to hold their own? In spite of their terrible losses, they had killed many of their wolfish foes. Numbers of them lay dead or dying. It would be small wonder if, after all, the rest should grow intimidated, and slink off. Yet after each temporary lull, there would be a fresh attack led by Shoomoo or Nitka, and again the air would ring with the terrible gathering cry of the packs.

At last the Indians could hold out no longer. Utterly unprepared as they were for this fearful horde of undreamed-of enemies; feeling, too, that their "medicine" had deserted them and that the Great Spirit, being offended, had abandoned them to their fate,—the survivors lost their presence of mind and fled shrieking down the hill.

Few, very few, ever found their way back to camp. It was the wolf triumph, the wolf revenge. The ridge, from end to end, was strewn with Indian dead.

It was Nitka herself who released Shasta, and her famous teeth which tore the thongs from his arms and legs, and, after long and patient work, at last set him free. And when he lay on the ground, almost too dazed to understand, with his whole body feeling like one big bruise, it was her loving tongue that comforted him, caressing him back to life.

The sun was already high in the heavens